REIGN

The Unwanted Series, Book II

C. M. NEWELL

REIGN, The Unwanted Series, Book II

An eBook Me Up Publication by arrangement with the author.

Copyright © 2020 by C. M. Newell

Cover Designer Maria Spada

Hard Cover Print ISBN: 9780997683660

Print ISBN: 9780997683639

eBook ISBN: 9780997683646

CONTENT WARNINGS

Bullying Behavior
Death, Murder

REIGN

TABLE OF CONTENTS

PART I

By knot of one, the spell's begun
By knot of two, it cometh true
By knot of three, so mote it be

My thoughts surface from the depths of a dark pool of nothingness. The first things I notice are the scent of rich earth and the feel of grass and dirt on the ground beneath me. These hold me steady. I smell smoke and hear the crackling of a campfire. I work to piece together my memory, a rush of blurry moments.

Barking. Duke is barking.

Smoke. A fire in the kitchen.

I'm yelling for Eoin, then being grabbed. My magick fails.

I'm being taken from my home. I fight, but there are more of them, and I'm in darkness; I can't see. I'm pushed, pulled—and then there's nothing left. My memories stop there.

I steady my breathing to avoid drawing attention. My first thought is of Rhydian, my royal Guardian, and blood-vowed protector. Should I reach out to him? That could make things worse, not knowing where I am. Rhydian would come armored with the rest of the royal armada, ready to kick butt. I shouldn't put any of them at risk until I know more. Heck, maybe I can escape on my own and get home.

Careful not to move my body, I squint my eyes to view my surroundings without alerting anyone that I'm awake. I don't hear anyone close to me. It's dark, but I can make out a campsite with a fire about ten meters away. The surrounding trees are tall and thick, more ominous than anything else, and possibly the best place to make a run for it. I make out some people—no, demons, with colorful skin and large horns that sweep back from their heads. There is no way for me to confirm where I am. It's possible that I'm still in Chepstow, Massachusetts, but I'm more likely in the magickal realm of Edayri. I open my eyes fully and confirm I am alone.

My body is stiff; my shoulder muscles scream because of the angle of my arms. Something weighs on my wrists behind my back. I'm still in my school uniform, the skirt twisted, but I can move my legs. I push against the heels of my purple chucks to sit up. The group near the campfire doesn't notice. A coldness comes over me. I've got to transport from here.

Holding my hands open behind my back, I mentally call my magick. I feel the familiar hum within me, but it won't rise beyond the surface. I twist to look over my shoulder and see the magick's familiar glow that should be flowing in patterns on my skin, instead contained in the glowing bracelets around my wrists.

I pull at the cuffs. My breathing is short and fast, and my eyes water as I attempt to shove the cuffs off. They don't move but instead pinch and twist on my skin. I yelp in pain. Someone at the fire turns my way.

I summon my magick again, then again.

Damn it, I need you!

I yank harder on the blasted bracelets and call to Rhydian in my mind. "Help me! Find me, please. They are coming!"

⚜

A jolt of pain travels up my arms in a snap. The connected cuffs release, and I can move my arms. The weight of each bracelet pulls my hands to my side as if each arm weighs ten pounds. My wrists glow like purple nightsticks. I could run, I think, or swing these heavy weighted bracelets at their heads. My magick shows itself on the surface of my skin more, but it's visibly muted and dull to my control; the patterns flow, ebb, pulse, and try to connect, but instead, the magick flows to these wicked bracelets!

Four young demons surround me; the opportunity to run into the trees is gone. These demons are dressed like anyone from my school, except they have colorful skin and small horns coming out of their heads. They keep a distance from me, observing the glowing bracelets.

A dark red female with short, black, spiky hair, wide dark eyes, and a taunting smirk gets closer to me. She's not so intimidating in her jeans, goth boots, and black anime hoodie.

"Your Royal Highness. You aren't much without it, are you?" She gestures to the glowing bracelets.

"Wanna test that?" I spit back, holding up the bracelets.

"Oh! So, you aren't helpless without your magick after all? How cute!" She claps her hands together, bats her eyes, and grins to reveal small fangs.

Cute? I'll show her cute when I use these heavy monstrosities on the side of her head!

The other three teenage demons move off to the side. A shorter male demon dressed in a dark track-suit, which I hadn't noticed earlier, moves closer in my periphery. I turn on him, and he jumps back a step.

"What do you guys want with me?"

The girl demon seems to be the only one talking. "To correct what you fucked up!"

"What I—?"

A deep rumble of a voice interrupts and captures our attention. A dark figure emerges from what appears to be a tent on the other side of the campfire. The horns are more substantial, not some teenagers. My heart pounds faster, and the chill of the air makes me shiver. The figure becomes familiar as it gets closer.

Theon.

CHAPTER 2

Theon is tall and lean, a cross between a grunge twenty-something and a samurai. He's a skilled fighter and usually near my uncle. Like my uncle, he is half Wiccan and half-demon.

His long hair is messy and obscures most of his face, but I can tell that his jaw drops at the sight of me. Marching in big strides, he focuses his attention on the feisty demon in front of me. "What the hell have you done, Sikkori?"

"We did what needs to be done. She's right here." Sikkori gestures to me with painted neon pink claws.

"No, you've complicated it more! The Guardians and the whole royal wiccan armada will be looking for her! Do you ever use your brain?" Theon pushes his hand through his hair and over his horns in visible frustration. He grabs Sikkori's arm and pulls her away. He points at the shorter demon to the side of me, who nods in some unspoken agreement.

"Please come with me and get warm by the fire,"

the shorter demon says in a small voice matched by a half-hearted smile. I follow him, watching Theon hover over Sikkori's tensed body.

I'm guided to sit on a large, fallen tree trunk. The childlike demon seems satisfied and gently touches my shoulder, almost bowing his head before he leaves.

He knows who I am and at least doesn't harbor the same irritation Sikkori seems to.

Theon raises his voice. "This camp location is in jeopardy now. It's not simple to just drop her off!"

Sikkori looks like a teen girl being scolded by a teacher. She rolls her eyes before pushing back. "So, she stays then!"

"And this is why. You asked. This is why you don't have more responsibility!"

Looking around, I see more tents scattered through the trees. I don't have a clear path to run. I give up on calling my magick; I can't use it because of the bracelets, and I can't seem to connect to Rhydian. I'm stuck.

I'm staring ahead, trying to formulate a plan when someone sits next to me. He's quiet and goes unnoticed by the few nearby because everyone is watching Theon and Sikkori. I know exactly who he is before I turn my head. This was the intel the Guardians had; this was why Sikkori brought me here.

Evan, my uncle, was presumably complete with the mental madness I caused by hitting him with magick during the battle at MacKinnon Manor.

He stares straight ahead like I'm not right next to him. I can't move. My uncle is . . . different. He's unkempt and messy, his eyes unfocused, nothing at all like himself.

I tentatively whisper his name. "Evan?"

The corner of his lip pulls up in recognition of his name. Without looking at me, he nods toward the arguing Theon and Sikkori. He waits until Theon throws his hands up in frustration, then speaks.

"Why is my niece here?"

Silence.

Theon walks in smooth strides to stand in front of Evan.

"Why is she here? No one said anything about this being the next step in our freedom, although plans do change."

Freedom?

"They just wanted to help you. The magick—" Evan holds his finger up, and Theon stutters before continuing: "Um . . . gift. The gift Willow gave you. They just want you . . . whole."

Sikkori hugs her body, looking younger. How old is she? I realize she must be younger than me at seventeen, although I feel like I've aged five years in several months since starting my senior year.

Evan doesn't respond. I break the uncomfortable silence. "Gift? What gift?"

"At the battle on the MacKinnon grounds, you sent uncontrolled magick that hit Evan. It was charged by your emotions, and it injured—ah, changed Evan."

Evan stands and sweeps his arms in a wide circle, spinning like a little child. "Freedom."

Everyone stares at Evan in the silence.

"The gift of seeing—understanding. The gift of redemption within myself and of knowledge. I hate, I love, I have anger and compassion, all rolled into one." Evan drops to one knee in front of me, and I scoot back, scraping the backs of my legs. I look everywhere but directly at his waiting face until he touches my knee. "It's freedom. I do not control it. It is only glimpses of the future. A wonderful gift from my niece."

I don't like this. How can I undo something I didn't know I was doing in the first place? What will they do to me if I make it worse?

"Ah, to be so young. Don't be burdened by the battle of doubt in your head," Evan says with a laugh. "No worries, Willow. I will keep my gift of sight, regardless of what the younger Emissaries' good intentions are."

"Emissaries?"

"Yes. That's us." Evan gestures in a big sweeping motion with his arms. Theon is assessing me with his scrupulous eyes.

I'm not sure what I should be more frightened of —the abduction to help Evan or the fact he doesn't want it. Either way, I'm limited with these bracelets.

Evan snaps his fingers, and the spellbinding bracelets break.

Did he just read my mind?

Evan offers his hand; I take it and stand. Theon rushes toward us, yelling for us to stop, and in a blur, he is gone. Evan is magickly transporting us. I gently pull my hand away, but I can't budge his steady grip. My feet land on solid ground and my stomach immediately turns with the abrupt guidance of the transport.

"Don't leave quite yet," Evan says, almost asking and hopeful.

Cold air sweeps around and chills me; the temperature is freezing. Cars sound in the distance. Though it is still dark, I can make out a colorful jungle gym among the dry winter grass. There are gravel walkways lined by leafless trees. Before I open my mouth, Evan waves his fingers and chants, covering me in warmth with new clothes—a thick puffed jacket, wool hat, and gloves. He has dressed for the cooler climate in a long, formal, black wool jacket and leather gloves. His horns, still visible, blend into his wavy hair.

"Why should I stay? Last time I saw you, Evan, I was collateral damage. Remember?"

"I wouldn't have."

I believe him, but it doesn't change the fact that the Guardians and Sabine don't believe that.

"Where are we, Evan? When can I leave?"

He squints and looks all around us, then stops and points over my shoulder. "Ah, there it is. Look."

The tip of the Eiffel Tower is a distant silhouette against the evening sky. So that's where we are. I have a sense of déjà vu that I can't connect.

"You were not born yet, when your parents took a stand against dear old dad. Later, I believe your father brought you here a few times." His smile turns from joy to sadness. "I needed to bring you away from the

Emissaries. I must protect them; the Horned God would want that. You also need to see and understand this place because of its ties to my sister. The history is important for you and your future, and for the Emissaries."

I have so many questions. I settle on the most immediate one. "Who are the Emissaries?"

"They are equality seekers."

"Who is the Horned God?"

"Quite simply, me." Evan laughs, and his horns glow just a little.

Okay . . .

"So, my Wiccan Queen and niece, what shall we do? Oh, yes—first, the warnings. Never run with scissors or knives unless your intention is to harm yourself and those around you."

He wobbles on his feet, and I back away with one big step. This is becoming even more strange than it already was.

"Evan? Are you okay? You seem . . ."

I can't bring myself to say it. Even's eyes, his face, look happy and carefree. He's different, but I'm different too. So much has happened since we first met under his guise of a therapist. He helped me connect to my magick and learn about my heritage. I look at him, and I long for my mother, my father, and the life that was normal—or more normal than this, anyway.

"So, do you recognize this place? Is it a place that calls to you, like a raven in another life?" He takes a deep breath and closes his eyes as if savoring the memory of something.

"Evan, why did you bring me here? It may be familiar, but I don't understand."

What's his intention? Is he going to let me go?

"We are tied together. Not physically, but the Goddess and the Horned God—we are their embodiment."

"How is that?" I breathe into my gloved hands and watch the chilled air turn white.

He laughs. "We are evolving and new." Evan waves his gloved fingers as if they are wings and his body moves by flutters in and out of my vision. "The caterpillar experiences the most evolution but its end result, the butterfly, has a lifespan that isn't very long."

What do I say? This is so weird.

"Remember this place, Willow. Ask Sabine about it. Consider what noble covens want and why. Don't be the status quo. Be a different Queen."

My mouth is dry. I don't know what to say to him. I want to be the right kind of Queen, but I can't be something I'm not. It strikes me that those teenage demons were worried about Evan. He's important enough they came for me and risked their lives. I could easily take the Guardians to them and have them all arrested or worse, but I won't do that. I can't do that.

"Call to Rhydian through your blood vow."

I need more from him besides my freedom. "Wait. Tell me more about this place before I leave. Why bring me here? How is it connected to my mother?"

He closes his eyes briefly. "This is where your father and mother took a stand against the Wiccan crown and the rule of betrothal. The place where we all flee toward a beacon of light." Evan points to the Eiffel tower in the distance and pulls his scarf closer to his neck. "The High Coven is not one to trust, but —" He laughs before continuing, his canines showing. "You already recognize that. Good girl. Don't let Sabine's perfect exterior fool you into thinking it mirrors an authentic interior. Chaos follows her—a type that is not only harmful but deadly."

I see it as soon as he says the word "deadly" his grief in a conjured vision of my mother and another lady I imagine was Meghan, his wife. She was killed by order of my grandfather, the Wiccan King, Evan's father. If it wasn't so cold and the light was better, I believe I would see tears gathering in his eyes.

"I'm sorry, Evan." I mourn as he does, for my mother, Mrs. Scott, and my father.

"You cannot have a funeral for someone without having a funeral for yourself." He shrugs, then says, "I'm sorry for all the losses we experience. Life is death, and death is life."

His eyes are haunted as they look everywhere but at me. Evan's weird riddles and words are true. I buried part of myself in the loss of my father, his death coming just as we were connecting, and he was sharing magick with me.

"Back into the mouth of the monster you go. Slay the dragon. If not, our time together may be brief."

His riddles sound like a threat and a warning at

the same time. The sincerity of his worry is something I don't doubt.

Who is the dragon I must slay?

Evan transports himself, his presence is gone too soon. Despite wanting to get home, I turn toward the jungle gym. He said so much that I don't completely understand, but the fact that this place is significant because of my parents gives me a reason to look around. I walk to a stone bench on the small greenway facing the jungle gym, pulling the collar of the coat closer to my neck. The cold wind whips my long hair and surrounds me in the quiet of the night.

A bronzed memorial plaque on the bench catches my eye. Summoning my magick to my fingers, I use the light to better see the inscription.

In memory of Nuala Warrington.

I remember so little of her. I take off my gloves and touch my mother's name as if that will bring me closer. I sit on the stone bench and tuck my hands into the warm pockets of the coat. I could easily transport myself home, but instead, I silent my mind and call to Rhydian as Evan directed me. I reach through space for the bond that connects us and comprehend his immediate connection and anguish.

The breeze on my face is instant. New warmth radiates from three royal Guardians who surround me in full armor and defensive stances.

Rhydian turns and I stumble to speak. "No one is here . . . um . . . besides me."

Cross's face drops from a scowl to a frown.

Tullen speaks first. "Willow, where have you been? It's been almost two days."

"I was taken by Emissaries and released by Evan, who took me here," I say with a shaky voice pointing to the plaque. Tullen reads it and touches my shoulder gently.

Rhydian hasn't moved. He's watching me as if he can't believe I'm in front of him. Finally, he speaks. "Cross, Tullen, search the park to see if there are any signs of magickal transport signatures."

"We arrived over there." I point to the spot where Evan brought us. "I don't think you'll be able to track him. Can we talk at my house? I just—want to go."

There is no verbal agreement, only Rhydian's outreached arms. The enveloping hug comforts me and releases the pit in my stomach. My tears fall without notice, and all I can do is breathe steadily in relief as Rhydian transports us to my front door in Chepstow, Massachusetts.

I don't release him, burying my wet face in his armored chest. Rhydian lifts my face gently to his and lays the sweetest kiss on my forehead. The moment is too brief. His forehead rests on mine in a physical and emotional connection that doesn't feel like a forced blood vow.

"I was so worried, Will. I couldn't sense you, and it was Evan all along. This could've been so much worse." Rhydian's statement is heavy on the cold night air.

"It was other Emissaries who grabbed me. Evan is

—different." How do I describe him without sounding crazy myself? I'm not even sure who to trust from his warnings.

"Why would you trust Evan? I don't care how different he seems; you agree he's partly responsible for Mrs. Scott and your father. Why are you wavering?"

The deaths of Mrs. Scott and my father are what Rhydian really wants to say—that Evan had a direct hand in what happened to my family. The twisted part is that Evan is my family. He's my uncle. Evan didn't kill anyone, Celestia did. She was responsible for Mrs. Scott's death and the torture and, ultimately, the death of my father. But I'm the killer that enacting justice on her. Deep down, when someone points out Evan's dark nature, I see that it mirrors my own—the dark voice I hear luring me from time to time.

"I don't believe Evan is a threat."

But do I really believe that?

CHAPTER 3

For a moment, I think Rhydian will leave me in the cold on the other side of the door. He purses his lips, his frustration palpable. Ever the gentleman—or maybe just adhering to his blood vow —he holds the door open and waits for me to walk in.

The foyer is unexpectedly crowded. Sabine, my long-lost grandmother, runs forward and hugs me hard. I stiffen and return the hug awkwardly.

Have we ever hugged before?

Evan's voice bounces in my mind, telling me to ask her about Paris, but I don't want the others around for that conversation. I keep it to myself.

The commander of the Guardians, Eoin, smiles and keeps his distance while watching Sabine continue to hold on to me.

"What happened?" Sabine asks. "Who did this? Are you okay?"

"Yes, I'm fine. It's okay."

"It most certainly is not okay for someone to enter

your home and forcefully take you from it. You, my dear, are Queen; this is not acceptable. I've spoken to Eoin. You will have more security here as long as you are to remain. We are putting up warded magick around the grounds of this house. No transporting in or out without warning." Her wide eyes are searching me, as if she is waiting for me to offer some accolade for her worry.

A tall, lean man enters the foyer from the stairs near the kitchen. He has a familiarity about him, but I don't recognize him. He strides forward gracefully, looking out of place in a formal navy pinstripe suit.

Sabine's attention gravities toward him, and she releases me. I'm grateful for the reprieve.

"Willow, allow me to introduce Mr. Esmund Boward. He represents the noble covens and is—"

"Your Majesty." He gives a bow so gracious it feels out of place for my home in Chepstow and my casual outfit. "I am also Rhydian's proud father and was a dear friend to your parents." He holds his hand out to me, palms up, waiting.

"Nice to meet you, Mr. Boward." I put my hand in his, and he holds it gently for a moment before releasing it. It's awkward.

"So, is the mystery of who abducted you solved?"

Before I can respond, Rhydian answers. "It was Evan."

The gasp from Sabine is audible, almost comedic. Is she putting on a show in front of Mr. Boward? Eoin is no longer leaning on the wall but at attention.

Clearing my throat, I look from Eoin to Sabine.

"Before you get carried away, it wasn't Evan directly. A group of demon teenagers abducted me."

"Demon teenagers," Sabine repeats, as if the idea is foreign.

"They are part of a group called the Emissaries? Their intention was for me to heal Evan. He was completely unaware of their plan. He—"

"Unlikely." Rhydian is quick to interrupt me. His expression is set in a challenge as if he wants me to change my mind just because he disagrees and the others side with him. Shaking my head, I stare hard at him. He is unmoving.

"Yes, quite." Mr. Boward agrees.

"Why would they want you to heal Evan? What is wrong with him?" Eoin asks, moving in to join the group that surrounds me.

Well, according to Evan, it's a gift. How do I describe that? I go for the most accessible explanation, knowing that I can tell Eoin more later. I have a feeling Rhydian will get to Eoin before me, per some official report to his commander, but Eoin lives with me in this house. Besides that, I trust him. I think he will be more objective than Rhydian and Sabine.

"He's very disheveled. His words don't always make sense—kind of like riddles, or that he has so many thoughts in his head he gets them confused as he speaks." My voice almost pitches to a question as I finish. This is not how I wanted to describe Evan. Everyone is waiting for me to explain more. "I don't know, he's just not what I'm used to seeing. They said I must have conjured an emotional magick into him when I fought him at MacKinnon Manor. I essentially caused this."

Cross smacks his large hands together in a loud clap. "All right then! Evan is incapacitated."

"No, he's not," I snap. Why am I defending him?

"Did you get a good look at the demons so that you can describe them?" Sabine asks.

"Not really."

The stare from Sabine is one of complete disbelief, but I continue, "I really don't think we should be going after a bunch of young teenage demons. Evan and Theon were not happy about it either. Anyway, I'm fine."

That did it, the roar of voices by saying Evan and Theon's names.

Thaxam, the demon general who I've added to the royal Guardians, shuffles his feet. Despite Ax's towering height and large red body, I didn't realize he was here until now. Eoin approaches Ax while Rhydian, Sabine, Cross, and Tullen talk over each other.

They are so engrossed in their arguments that no one notices me go to the stairs and take a seat near Ax and Eoin, except maybe Rhydian.

Mr. Boward's voice booms over the commotion. "It is unacceptable that someone came into this home, protected as it was, and removed the Queen against her will. This will not be viewed favorably by the noble covens. Her Majesty's ability to reign will be under question if it is not already. She should make her permanent home in Edayri at her ancestral estate of Mackinnon Manor. There is no reason to stay here."

Why is he trying to manage me? I'm tired, and nothing is going to happen tonight—or is it almost morning? Eoin begins to argue. I stand and interrupt.

"Thank you for your concern, but this is my and Sabine's decision. The agreement is to maintain my home and schooling here in Chepstow until the summer. This arrangement is supported by the Guardians. Eoin continues residency for the short term of this assignment."

Sabine is at my side. Her arm around my shoulders, awkward again, as if to show a united front. "Esmund, it has been a long day. We can discuss this later. For now, a report should be made that the Wiccan Queen is safe and sound in her family home."

As if a game is afoot, Mr. Boward's sly grin creeps across his face. "I'm glad that if the Queen is staying here, the Guardian's agreement on Rhydian's presence at her scholastic institution will be enacted. This will be important for her safety as well as that of the others who attend—" his voice hitches before he finishes "—like mortals."

"What?" My eyes snap to Eoin. I feel heat flush my face. Arrangements about my safety are being discussed without my knowledge. Rhydian didn't even say anything to me. Was this done ahead of my disappearance?

Eoin turns from me to place himself in front of Mr. Boward. He's the same height as Mr. Boward, and his presence alone is substantial. Eoin's tone is direct and low. "Mr. Boward, the Queen's security, is not a political or gossip tidbit for you to discuss. If you cannot maintain royal confidentialities, I will see that you are removed from consultation as the noble coven representative."

Eoin turns to me before continuing. "Rhydian has enrolled at Trinity Cross High and will be in several of your classes." Rhydian does not look at me, but he doesn't have to. I can sense his agreement on this arrangement.

"Are you serious?" They can't really think this is a good idea. As if I can't be alone at school? This is so ridiculous.

"Willow, Rhydian isn't but a couple of years older than you. He can pass as a student at your school. No one will question it," Sabine says, confirming her agreement with Eoin. Before my temper ignites, she quickly adds, "This doesn't change that you will split your time between here and Edayri. You will have a set schedule for training—you did agree to this, after all. This is the most normal we can give you while ensuring your safety and that of others."

This is far beyond ordinary, but I'm not ready to give up this little slice of my life. I say my goodnight and slowly climb the stairs as the rumble of discussions continue without me.

Staring down the school hallway, I watch my best friend and ex-boyfriend, Lucy and Daniel, like a voyeur. I recognize their new-couple dance—the shoulder touch, the lean in, the smiles and laughter. Realizing how creepy I am watching them, I give it up to walk to homeroom. They are moving toward a future that I don't get to belong to. I'm happy for them and comforted that Daniel isn't caught up in my royal mess of a life. It wasn't long ago that he was on death's door at my house. I don't regret breaking up with him; his life is on the path it should be on.

Homeroom is faster than my reverie of internal thoughts. The bell rings and lifts my mental fog, dismissing us to first period. We spill into the hallway, the class breaking up to go their separate ways. Coral and her cronies pass, giggling. They are gossiping and fanning themselves in dramatic teen girl fashion. Emily rolls her eyes as we walk toward them.

"What the heck is Coral all excited about? A new Tiffany color or something?" Emily asks.

A girl nearby overhears. "Ah, the new transfer. I mean, whoa!"

Emily, ever the flirt, turns to look for the student who is causing the girls to overheat, but I already know.

She spots him. "Oh, it's just—"

"Rhydian," I finish without looking.

"Yeah. Although I've got to say, he does brighten up the school a bit with his GQ quality looks." I grimace, but Em continues without a beat. "If you're into that sort of thing." Her smile is infectious, and she nudges me in my side.

"This is different and you know it," I say in a whisper.

Walking in, I go to my seat in the back near the window. He walks in seconds later. I guess I can't put this off any longer. It's happening—Rhydian is attending my school and my classes. "Hey," I say, waving.

Everyone is watching, most notably Coral with squinted eyes.

"Hey, Willow. I knew you went here. How fortunate we're in class together."

"I know, shocking." I try not to sound overly sarcastic and work to keep from rolling my eyes, but it's bubbling on the surface. I've never been a good actor.

The bell rings and class begins. I am trying my hardest only to watch Mrs. Gunter, but every time

Coral turns her head to spy Rhydian, I can't help but look her direction.

This is all we need—a triangle conflict between me, Coral, and Rhydian. Haven't we traveled this road before? Coral, Daniel, and me? Rhydian is not just any guy. I don't like the idea of her flirting and pursuing him. Her gossipy nature will not keep anything under wraps where I'm concerned.

After class, Rhydian is slow to leave, waiting for me.

"Are you in my next class as well?" I try not to snap.

"Can we not be seen together?"

I roll my eyes at him.

"That hurts Willow. And yes, of course, we are in all the same classes except two."

We leave together. Coral is waiting just outside the door to pounce on Rhydian. She clears her throat. "Welcome to Trinity Cross and Chepstow." Did her voice just raise two octaves? She's shifting her weight back and forth.

"Yea, thanks. You're Coral, right?"

Why did she giggle at her own name?

"Yes. I was curious if you'd like to get to know some of your fellow students—"

"Hey guys!" Emily interrupts, bouncing in and hanging her arm over Rhydian's shoulder. "Plans today, right, Rhy? Plus, you know our little tribe."

Coral stares hard at Emily before focusing back on Rhydian, her smile plastered. "Maybe another time then."

Saved by the bell, but not before she touches Rhydian's arm in a too-comfortable gesture.

Laughing, he catches up to me. "Boy, she really gets under your skin, huh?"

Oh, he has no idea. It's not just me. Or is it? I shrug. Whatever.

It doesn't take me long to realize that the only classes Rhydian's not in are the ones I share with Marco or Emily. Smooth, Eoin. Very smooth. The air I breathe at school is weighed, measured, and totally secured. It's suffocating if I think about it too hard.

At the end of the school day, when I can finally breathe in my own car, Rhydian surprises me by jumping in the passenger seat. He slings his dark backpack onto the back seat. He fits well in school. In the school uniform, he seems younger than the Guardian warrior he really is.

"So, are my friends, my keepers, as well? Emily and Marco? This is so wrong! I don't need a babysitter."

"I'm not your babysitter. I'm your protector and royal Guardian. Very different." His smile disarms me, but I focus on driving out of the school parking lot and toward home. "I don't get this. It isn't as if I don't have magick at my fingertips. It's insulting that Sabine and Eoin are interfering at school. And this was decided without even talking to me! What's with that!"

I realize I'm speeding and being aggressive in traffic. Rhydian grabs the overhead handle on the door.

"What? Don't like my driving, either?" I smirk.

"I'm sure you'll have to be my chauffeur before too long."

He laughs, relaxed. "Maybe because your driving skills are equivalent to those of the elderly."

"Are you kidding me right now?"

He lifts an eyebrow and his mouth quirks. I push my car's speed and turn the wheel hard on the street, heading west toward the house. The two-lane road is smooth and empty, the black tar glistening in the afternoon sun. I floor it.

My BMW grabs the road like the premiere car it is. My smile widens, and I weave, testing the grip of my tires—Rhydian rocks in his seat with a wide grin. The tall trees speed by us in a blur of green.

"Okay, okay. What do they say here—speed kills?"

Laughing with him, I pull into the driveway. I exhale the air from my lungs and turn to Rhydian. "I'm sorry."

"You'll resent me if you think I'm your captor from freedom. Can you look at this as us getting to spend more time together instead?"

I nod. He's right. I shouldn't lash out at him; he's doing his job. Wow. What a jumbled web of "have to," "ordered to," and "want to."

"Sorry," I say, "but if you say Coral is pretty or nice, I will blow up!"

"So, you're jealous?"

I return his playful grin but don't respond. Instead, I tease him before going into the house. My control in any part of this situation is my ability to make the most of it.

Light from the windows bathes the foyer when I wander downstairs later. In my father's office, I find Tullen and Quinn on security detail. They are seated at the curved game table by the window playing a high-stakes game of chess. Father once told me that he would sit with his father at the game table every Sunday and play various strategy games. I should have done this more with my father.

"Hi, Willow. What's the plan this evening?" Quinn asks, moving his knight.

"Just relaxing. A 'welcome back' day, as far as I understand. Although Tullen, maybe you have something else planned?"

Tullen scratches his red beard, studying the chessboard. He finally settles on moving a rook that takes one of Quinn's. "How about you play the winner? I'm finding this game to be quite a challenge."

"I've never learned to play."

They both look at me, stunned.

"What? It wasn't something I had an interest in before."

Quinn, without studying the board, moves a piece that captures a pawn. "Check."

Tullen laughs in a jovial way that shakes his top knot bun. "Well, it looks like we could both use a lesson in this game of strategy. Quinn, would you indulge me in another round?"

Quinn smiles and sets up the board. "Sure. You're getting better, and what's another game?"

"I'll leave you to it."

I wander into my father's secret coven room behind the office bookcase. Entering the room, I inhale the familiar scent of him—spices mixed with lush forest. The room illuminates with candles and lamps at my presence; the green paisley print, overstuffed chair calls to me from the last time I was here. The bookcase and its cabinets hold books about magick and history alongside various spices, roots, and other liquids with handwritten labels from my father and mother. The table against the wall displays only a small metal bowl and a stone pestle and grinder.

I think about my father's words about dark and light magick. I am a combination of both—my father's very dark magick and my mother's light magick—although I realize I'm more connected to my father since accepting his magick at his passing. He had said magick is simply magick, but at times I wonder if it's influencing. I find more temptation in my thoughts to do something cruel. I did take vengeance on Celestia without much thought. Was I justified in doing so, since it was her order to kill Mrs. Scott and my father? These thoughts can overwhelm me, although I try not to dwell on them. But seeing Evan . . . I did that to him. Maybe what I did was a gift, but the fact is, I did it without much thought. I was hurting and wanted him to hurt just as bad.

I sink into the overstuffed chair and pull my family's Book of Shadows into my lap.

Flipping through the Book of Shadows, I ask, "How strong is my father's magick's heritage?"

On a blank page, a family tree that starts with a noble coven member, William Warrington Senior, begins to appear. The lines and squares connect, and toward the bottom of the page, my father's name is written in a scripted font. Aiden Warrington. The ink continues and sketches portraits of each person. My father's portrait is of him as an older teen. I touch the familiar face with my fingertip as if to really touch him. A welling tear escapes, and I wipe it away quickly with the back of my hand.

Taking a shaky breath, I ask the book, "Am I fit to be Queen?"

The answer appears within seconds on the page.

Cannot predict now.

I chuckle at the response, remembering the day my father told me about my mother and the gift our family Book of Shadows has with magic eight ball responses. As my mother drifts into mind, so does Evan and Paris.

If I dive into the question, do I really want the answer? I've lost everything for a crown that was inherited. I can't help the nagging feeling that knowing will pull me further from my normal life— my life before the start of the school year, one where there was no magick or royal crown, even if "normal" was secretive and flawed.

I square my shoulders and ask, holding two fingers to the empty page. "Paris. Is it important to my family? Or to who I am?"

The ink on the page swirls around my fingertips at first, then grows in big loops that suddenly dissolve into the thickness of the paper. Lifting my fingers, I exhale and lay my head back into the chair, staring blankly ahead.

A movement on the page brings my attention back, and I stare at the response.

As I see it, yes.

So, I'm not playing into some bigger plot at Evan's hands?

My sources say no.

I didn't ask another question while touching the page, did I? I trace the unmoving words. "Why?"

Better not tell you now.

"Well, you have to now," I say, as if I'm confronting a friend who evasively answers questions with non-answers.

Outlook not so good.

The Book of Shadows is sassy. Great, just what I need.

The words begin to morph again without me touching the page.

Without a doubt.

I'm not sure which thought this response actually answers. I suppose the book is much better than an actual magic eight ball, and I should be relieved I am getting some type of answer.

"Will you always be available to me to answer questions?"

Ask again later.

As I touch the page, the words sink into the paper

and disappear. I don't have any other questions besides major ones that need more than a three-word reply. Those I'll save for Sabine. This is going to be difficult, but at least the Book of Shadows is not judging me.

As I see it, yes.

Great.

CHAPTER 5

I t's Friday, but I'm not at Trinity Cross High
School. Instead, I'm in Edayri for a different type
of education: physical training, royal business, and
etiquette.

The joy of being me.

I think I would rather be in Mrs. Simpson's
Organic Chemistry class, which is saying something.
Sabine and Mr. Boward insisted that I spend Fridays
in Edayri because my weekends are not enough for me
to assimilate my royal duties. Like I have any time to
myself anymore. How am I supposed to have a normal
life if I'm not home on the weekends?

Wiping the sweat from my brow, I try to stay in
the present by funneling my frustration into magickal
sparring. Eoin is shouting commands and instructs me
while I face off with Rhydian in the Guardian private
gym. Usually, Cross is my opponent.

"Are you intimated? Come on. Attack," Rhydian
says, wiggling his brows and bouncing around the mat

like a boxer. He's moving like we haven't been here for over a half-hour.

"No. I'm not intimated." I'm appreciative of his muscled frame. And yes, I'm a little intimated.

"Okay then, attack."

Cross would have already taunted and yelled at me to get under my skin and invoke a response. In his absence, I think about Sabine and how my freedoms are slowly slipping from me.

Magick flows like liquid across my skin. I pull it from my arms and lift my hands to ignite a flame mid-air. Rhydian is moving his hands in a shielding pattern as he takes a defensive stance. I guide the fire forward at Rhydian, but he catches me off guard by ducking and rolling toward me. I jump back, and the flame disappears along with my footing. As I fall, I sweep Eoin's legs even though he's only observing. He goes down with me.

Eoin doesn't stop training me from the floor. "As your power builds within your body, your goal is to control your thoughts, so they become actions with the outcome you desire," Eoin says. He has said this to me almost weekly since I've known him. It drives me nuts. As if I could forget with him always harping on about it. "Are you rolling your eyes at me? That's not very royal of you."

"I controlled my graceful fall into complete action. Your ass is down just like mine."

"Funny," Eoin responds dully, but the smirk on his face says something else. He's not just the commander of the Guardians; he's also my parental Guardian and the reason I can stay at school in Chepstow. For that, I am so grateful. He's like an adopted father figure in my life.

I laugh and lay back into the mat, one sweaty mess. Rhydian chuckles under his breath before giving me his hand to help me up.

"Apologies. Now should I conjure a light ball to throw at your head?" I ask playfully.

Eoin holds up his finger and taps his earpiece. "Yes? I understand. Be there in five."

Eoin stands to leave. When Rhydian and I stare at him waiting for directions, he says, "Go ahead and wrap it up. You've got twenty minutes before etiquette training. Your instructor will meet you at MacKinnon Manor in the royal sitting room by the gardens."

I nod, feeling grateful as Eoin leaves the room. A break. Finally.

Sweat trickles down my back, sticking to my shirt. "Want to shower?"

My jaw drops open. I close my mouth, open it to respond, close it again, and try not to look like a fish.

"By the blush on your face, I can tell you thought I meant together. I didn't mean that initially, but if you would like, I'm happy to please the Queen in whatever way I can." A smirk highlights the deep dimple in Rhydian's cheek.

Damn, he's so handsome and appealing even sweaty. "Yes, I do need that shower, although I may take a rain check on the other." Did I just say that out loud? Where is this confidence coming from? Goddess, I want to hide under a rock.

"Rain check?"

"It's a saying for another time. Besides, I don't think Eoin or Sabine would approve." I'm an idiot. Switching subjects, I go for the question that's been weighing me down lately. "Can you tell me more about the blood vow?"

Rhydian comes forward and takes my hands in his. My heart beats loudly in my ears; my skin tingles touching him. It feels natural and straightforward, and simultaneously it is anything but. I like the way my hands fit in his, despite that they are slick with sweat.

"The blood vow that I made to your father was one of protection and duty. Part of that vow provides an instinctual magick that allows me to be what and where you need. It's not something any Guardian takes lightly, as the vow connects you for life. The only exceptions are if I break the vow by causing physical harm to you or if the recipient releases you, although I hear that if you are released, it can be painful beyond measure for both in the vow. That's not a common thing. Usually, the vow is beneficial to both parties."

I think my world is rocked. How can he make a vow like this without knowing me? A one-sided vow. The desire to kiss him nags at me, and I push it to the side. "But you have control over what you do, right?"

"A vow didn't tell me to hold your hand."

My hands slip from his, and I'm aware of the

instant loss, the connection of his touch. He reaches back for them.

"See?"

"Not really. You felt a need to hold my hand?"

"You needed me to comfort you. You wanted a physical—how do I describe it? A physical connection, but you're not committed, so I held your hand."

I pull back my hands and step away from our closeness. I'm completely embarrassed that he can sense my attraction to him. How is that possible, besides my beet-red face? Is he forced to do anything to comfort me? "So, what you're saying is you're compelled then? Is that it?"

"Exactly." He smiles.

I'm now something to be obeyed? He doesn't seem upset by this at all. Is he brainwashed? Am I? I want him. Oh crap. This is wrong! He should be moved by himself, not by me. This is one-sided. I want to scream at him, but he's a grinning like a happy puppy dog.

"Unbelievable!" I snap. I grab my bag, slinging it behind my back.

"What? Why are you—angry?"

"Are you serious?" I turn on him and catch him off guard. In my head, shout, "Kneel before me now!"

He smiles and begins to take a knee.

I point to his action before he reaches the floor. "That is why!"

"You just told me to—"

"Argh!" I turn away from him. "I'll see you later, Rhydian."

Realizing I have one-sided power over him, that even when I command him in my head, he obeys, I scream in frustration in the hallway. He can sense my emotions, wants, and needs, and this vow is a command. I can literally command him in my mind!

Some rational part of my mind reminds me that, as Queen, I can command anyone.

Are his feelings toward me even real? Or am I transferring my feelings in a way that commands him?

CHAPTER 6

I'm late, but no one is in the office suite. I take a seat at the window that overlooks the well-manicured grounds of MacKinnon Manor. My eyelids are heavy, and my mind is quiet for the first time. My eyes are almost shut when a male voice grabs my attention.

"I'm sorry to disturb your reprise. I was detained with noble coven matters." Mr. Boward walks with long strides and places his leather-bound notebook and fancy pen on the table in front of me.

"Are you my teacher? I wasn't sure who to expect for this lesson."

He looks very similar to his son in height and coloring, but not in facial features. His nose is rather large and screams aristocrat.

"Yes. I will be your guide through all things royal, per etiquette, and other miscellaneous expectations as it were. I hope I can be of assistance to you as you adjust."

"I thought Sabine would be showing me the royal ways," I say, using air quotes around the word royal.

"Lady MacKinnon continues other royal work in your absence by reviewing and signing various decrees as your proxy." He straightens his suit lapels before sitting in front of me. "I would surmise that she wants to be more of your grandmother in her free time than anything else."

That's kind of him to say, but the fact that he isn't looking at me gives me the feeling there is something more to his statement. There is something about him, an air of superiority that is off-putting.

"Well, let us start, shall we?"

He starts to open the notebook, then closes it. "Maybe we should start by getting acquainted with one another. You may not be aware, but I was close friends with your mother and father. We all grew up together."

My father never mentioned him, but he did go to him and Rhydian for this blood vow. I can't believe my father did that—tie me to someone I didn't know without talking to me. Then again, when it comes to my protection, it seems like something he'd do. I also have a hard time seeing my father being good friends with Mr. Boward. Then again, it wasn't as if I met any close friends of his before. Everyone I ever met was a colleague or some finance titan. I want to like Rhydian's father, but he reminds me of the elite who look down on everyone and only do things to support their agendas. The judgment in his eyes is a reminder that I'm not like him. I'm sure others like him would probably prefer a more refined elite sitting at the Wiccan throne.

"I wasn't really aware that you knew my parents. How long had you been friends with my father? When did he go to you regarding the blood vow?"

"It does seem like a long time ago, even though it's only been a few months. I think your father had some suspicions last summer; he reached out to me and we discussed various options. I proposed the blood vow to your father. With Rhydian's captain ranking in the Guardians, it was a good choice."

How easily he would offer up his son for a blood vow that links him for life. Did Rhydian not even have a choice in the matter? "What other options were up for discussion? Was this all about my safety?"

Mr. Boward shifts in his chair and leans closer to me. The look of sympathy in his eyes is off-putting. "Willow, you are your father's greatest treasure. He would do anything to protect you. Having a Guardian in the position that Rhydian is in puts you in the safest hands possible. The crown is heavily sought after, especially unclaimed. The realization that keeping you from Edayri put you at a disadvantage meant that you needed protection by someone who grew up here. From there, it became apparent that there was only one choice."

I mutter something about the word "choice" under my breath.

"And trust me, Rhydian had a choice. He chose duty and sacrifice. It is an honor for him and our family to serve a royal." I'm stuck on the word sacrifice. I elicit sacrifice from people for my wellbeing? I never thought of it that way. It's a lot to absorb. "Our ways may seem antiquated and different, but they are traditional and at the root of Wiccan laws. They will take some time to understand, and I am happy to provide guidance on your journey. Sabine has been kind enough to appoint me to the position of Scepter to you and crown interests."

Why do I get the feeling that handling me is his new position? What is Sabine doing? I don't need extra handling, I have enough of that.

"Mr. Boward—"

"Please, call me Esmund. May I, in turn, call you Willow?" His smile is strained.

"Oh absolutely, please call me Willow or Will." The look on his face suggests I've gone a little too far with the informal response and nickname. "Okay, Willow, it is. Thank you, Mr.—sorry, Esmund, for the time to get more acquainted with you."

"My pleasure, dear. Our family is here for your service. It is a great honor."

Esmund stands and touches my shoulder, which sends chills straight to my spine. Sabine's voice echoes into the room from the hall outside. She sweeps in full of grand style in a skirt that fans out with her steps and her hair streaming behind her in long red waves.

"Oh, Esmund, wonderful to see you as always. I hope today's lesson went well. However, I must cut the time short. Willow has crown business to work through this evening with me. It's come to my attention that dinner will be ready soon, and somehow the day has passed too quickly."

Thankful for Sabine's timing, Esmund says his goodbyes and quickly leaves. Sabine and I enter the formal dining room where only two places are set.

"I hope you don't mind the change of scenery, but I do love this room and the open stone fireplace. I find it relaxing, and I need to get away from the various office suites in this Manor. Some days my home does not feel like my home at all; it is more like a company office space."

"I totally understand," I reply. The dining room is welcoming with its dark wood table and high back chairs. The room is rich in maroons and purples, the low light coming from the fire warm.

There is no time wasted as we eat dinner. Sabine talks me through the procession of decisions that have already been made regarding arrests and incarcerations of other creatures. I'm not really clear on all the particulars, but it certainly seems that Edayri is experiencing unrest with various crimes. The crown role of delivering any type of sentence to anyone is uncomfortable. At the same time, I have no idea how to push back with Sabine.

"Are all of the crimes being committed confirmed? Are there trials?"

Sabine chuckles as she takes a sip of her wine. "Willow, trials are something that would've been a part of the High Coven that you disbanded, but only for high crimes against the crown. These misdemeanors and the lower-level creatures who perform them are under your jurisdiction for judgment."

"That is completely unfair. How am I supposed to pass judgment on someone else? I don't know what the laws are and how to go about that. Isn't there something in place for this type of thing?"

"Which is why I do this, as a proxy until you are comfortable and trained on all your royal duties. You may read over each plea and change the order as you wish; however, I have taken it upon myself to stay within the current Wiccan tradition in all judgments. I highly encourage you to remain consistent in these ways."

I feel the heat rise all around me. Embarrassment at not knowing the laws and frustration of expectation makes a heady mix. I sorely don't like being told what to do. I want to respect this tradition, but I'm turned off by thinking that the laws are only beneficial to Wiccans.

"Also, we might as well extend your stay for the week. A lot is going on regarding these crimes that I feel may be a threat to you directly. It's not just Evan or the Emissaries, it seems. We need to show unity and strength."

"Sabine, we can show unity and strength, but our agreement is our agreement. I will be going to high school during the week."

"You do realize how superfluous this is—high school nonsense in the Terra realm. Your job will be here. Your family, your responsibility, your duty is here in Edayri."

"You do realize that my life is in Chepstow, Massachusetts. That is my home, the Terra realm. It isn't something I'm giving up."

"If you would only consider—"

"You have Rhydian attending school with me. Isn't that enough for now? I'm here until the end of the weekend."

Sabine huffs in resignation. She finally nods and takes a long drink of her wine. Of course, I will continue next week at my high school.

I doubt many of my friends would have argued so heavily to stay at school. I have lost my mind.

CHAPTER 7

I t's my third day in my MacKinnon Manor room, which is more like an apartment than an actual bedroom. The decor is neutral with light browns and creams. The dark wood of the furniture matches that throughout the rest of the manor. The only patterned items are the rug and cream curtains. It's as if I'm a guest in a penthouse hotel. I even have a sitting room with a large fireplace and couches, and a closet the size of my room back home. It's overwhelming. Too big, too much.

When I'm in Edayri, the one thing I'm connected to is my cell phone. It has been enchanted so that I can text my friends in Chepstow. It was the one thing Eoin did for me, despite turning the enchantment into a lesson. Needless to say, I'm grateful for the connection.

I'm using that connection now as I lay on my four-poster bed, texting Emily. I tell her that Rhydian is showing me around Edayri tonight. Strictly speaking, it wasn't part of my training schedule coordinated by Sabine, though she did put it in my calendar later.

So, it's a date!

I hesitate. Rhydian's idea and he didn't attach any work formality to it, but . . .

I don't know if I can call it a date.

And why not? An outing planned by the two consenting parties is a date bonehead. Emily responds.

My stomach churns. Leave it to Emily, call things the way they are.

I guess so. Now I'm nervous.

Her response is immediate. *Oh yeah, it's a date.*

This is complicated, he's a royal Guardian, there's this whole blood vow thing, and this is a date?

Girl, you like him, just go with it and get out of your head.

She's right. I should just go with it; there are too many things weighing down on me anyway. This could be what I need to escape—just being a normal teen girl with a crush. Damn it, I'm so stupid—of course, this is a date, regardless of Sabine recording it in a calendar like a task.

Emily proceeds to tell me exactly what to wear. I completely ignore her. I have no idea where we are going or what we are doing, but I know it will be here in Edayri, and I don't want to be the crown. My goal is to be myself, just Willow, with no title or motive. Therefore, no dresses or skirts. I smile as I pick out an outfit—shiny black jeggings, a dark gray V-neck sweater with a purple tank underneath, my mother's necklace tucked into my shirt and black flats. I check myself in my full-length mirror. I pull my hair out of its twist ponytail and shake it out, catching a whiff of my lavender shampoo as the long waves cascading past my shoulders. I swipe on some lip gloss and mascara and smile, feeling my heart swell with happiness.

I'm going on a date with Rhydian.

Yara, a familiar house staff member, knocks on my door and announces that Captain Rhydian Boward is waiting for me in the formal foyer downstairs. I thank her and grab my black coat. I take the stairs two at a time and try not to run down the small hall that leads to the foyer. The thought replays through my mind over and over: I'm going on a date with Rhydian.

Like a regular date, Rhydian is waiting in the foyer without Guardian armor on. He's dressed in dark jeans and a navy peacoat. His wavy dark hair is tamed tonight, and he's cleaned up the smooth undercut around his ears and neck. His hazel eyes sparkle as he smiles. My heart races when he reaches for my hand, and my stomach does a little jump when I close my fingers around his.

"Ready to discover the homeland?" he asks.

"Yes. Am I dressed okay for where we are going?"

"I think so. Sorry, I should've been clearer about what we are doing tonight. I think being a little inconspicuous might be nice for you to observe Edayri as it is rather than as people would like the crown to imagine it."

"Perfect."

Walking out of MacKinnon Manor, I breathe in the crisp twilight air, and my anxiety melts away. Emily is right; I need to get out of my head and be in the present. That is my entire goal for tonight.

Rhydian escorts me to a car, the likes of which I have never seen before. It's some type of convertible sports car that sits low to the ground, dark with an iridescent blue and purple sheen that shimmers in the light of the manor's gas lamps.

Rhydian opens the door opens for me. I sit and look for a seat belt that isn't there.

"There are a few differences in our vehicles. Don't worry, it's safe. Besides, we have nowhere near the amount of traffic you do."

I laugh. "That is definitely something I wish we had." I wait until he takes his seat before asking, "So, where are we going?"

"I thought it would be nice to drive to the Lunar Falls. This way, you can appreciate the landscape and see where magickal water flows to Edayri."

The lush green forest that expands well beyond MacKinnon Manor is impressive. The thick trees and twilight sky intermingle in hues of blue and green. I love the winding road and constantly changing view. Everything is perfect and breathtaking.

Rhydian breaks me away from my daydreaming. "Tell me what you're thinking."

I start. "Wait, you don't know? Can't you read my mind or something?"

"No, I only sense emotions that come through,

and I'm still getting to understand yours. I can't read your mind, Willow." He grins. I smile back.

"Nothing. Taking in the scenery. It's beautiful."

Looking at me intently, he grins. "Yes, it is."

The words to flirtatiously respond are lost in my throat; my confidence is suddenly hidden. Instead, I smile back, meeting his eyes only for a moment before shyly turning back to watch the trees pass us by in thick green lines.

We come upon the biggest tree I have ever seen, the trunk is split and straddles the road as if it was made that way, and we drive through it. The moon shines brighter on the other side of the tree. The moon is on the right side of us, and it looks like an unreal, a liquified reflection in various shades of white that extend unnaturally on the ground as if it's part of the water off to the side of the road. Is the moon feeding the water? I almost feel as if I could touch the stars. Rhydian pulls the car off the road onto unpacked gravel.

"From here, we walk." He opens my door before I can figure it out myself and takes my hand. When I stand, I'm close to him. The space between us is electric. My magick hums lightly, and I hold it in so that it doesn't show on my skin. He leads me toward a dirt path I hadn't seen before.

"Rhydian, tell me something about you."

"Like what?"

"Whatever you'd like to share. I dunno. I guess I'd like to know you better outside of work."

"Aw, Willow, happy to talk about anything inside

or outside of work. Let's be clear—tonight is definitely not work."

My heart and magick rise together in a beat. Tonight is not work. I am not a task.

We arrive at the edge of a tree-lined path that leads toward a slope. I assume that this will guide us to the body of water we came to see. "So, tell me about your family then. Your dad—he seems to be fairly close with Sabine and quite important with the noble covens."

Rhydian's eyes grow a little somber at the mention of his father. "He's an ambitious man for sure, and strictly one for tradition. He's quite prideful. He raised me and my older sister, Abigail. My mother left when I was younger."

"I'm sorry about your mother."

His smile is quick, but the sorrow behind his eyes shows. We come over a ridge, and the lake comes into sight. He leads me to a spot in the grass near the water, and we sit. "We have quite a bit in common," he says, "with regard to mothers. Although yours didn't choose to leave."

My heart aches for him. I'm not sure what to say, so I just sit next to him at the edge of the lake and lay my head on his shoulder.

"You'd like Abby. She's spunky like you. It drives my father crazy."

"Is that your nice way of telling me that I drive your father crazy?"

"I would never reveal such a thing," he says, then laughs, giving away the truth.

"Do you ever see your mother?"

"No. Actually, she's in the Terra realm like you. I remember visiting her when I was about seven years old. It isn't something I've ever pursued. Hard for me to pursue her when she left is us so easily."

There is no anger in his voice, but I feel something from him—a hint of sadness. I hold his hand and squeeze it gently. He responds in kind.

"Do you hear that?" he asks after a moment.

I listened intently, but I don't hear anything except the wind sweeping through the tall grass and reeds at the water's edge. Then, almost buried by the wind, I hear something like a whistle. The faint sound draws my attention.

"Maybe? What am I listening for?"

Rhydian stands, still holding my hand, and pulls me to my feet. He puts his finger to his lips, and we inch behind the very tall reeds. Rhydian points to where the moon reflects on the water. He smiles. I follow his eyes, not sure where to focus.

"Fairies," he whispers.

I look closer, knowing that fairies reveal themselves in various ways. Being the small creatures they are, they mostly shield themselves; that's what I remembered from a book Tullen gave me. I find them at last, shimmering like the moonlight. There are about a dozen of them playing in the light on the water. If I listen carefully to the whistles and rings, I recognize a sort of music. Their wings flutter and pause in a way that makes it look like they were dancing. They interlock their arms and kick their legs in unison. I stare, amazed. I've never seen anything like this before.

Rhydian moves one of the tall reeds for us to get a better view, but this alerts the fairies, and they disappear by extinguishing their lights. Only a few continue to glimmer, curious. One bold male dressed in suspenders moves closer toward us, heedless of the squeaks of warning behind him.

"Hello," I say in a very small whisper, hoping not to scare him. "I'm sorry if I interrupted. I was curious when I heard your song and saw your dance."

Rhydian stays still behind the reeds, but the fairy does not miss a beat. He points at Rhydian. I smile and shrug my shoulders. "He's with me."

The fairy seems unimpressed with my apology but continues to point at Rhydian. "Rhydian?" I ask.

"I'm afraid he is aware that I'm a Guardian. I believe we've met before."

When I look back at the fairy, he is on one knee bowing to me. The fairies who were behind him are now unshielded and also bowing. They recognize who I am, but I don't want a scene, and I don't want them to treat me differently.

"I'm sorry I've interrupted you. May I join your party?" I circle my finger and draw a light circle in the air, similar to what they were doing on the water.

The fairy smiles and the other fairies come to life. Lights twinkle all around like fireflies.

"Thank you." I turn to Rhydian with a questioning look. Why did they change their manners so quickly?

"The fact that you apologized and asked was beyond their expectations of you as Queen. You honored them, and fairies take this highly. Besides, most of them look like they are a bit drunk from the party."

I laugh, seeing a few stumble into the water.

The music gets louder, and the fairies begin dancing and laughing and kicking up water all around in tiny splashes. Amidst all the fun, I spy my reflection, the crown on my forehead ebbing and flowing with my magick. The fairies don't seem to care as they continue with their party. Rhydian claps his hands together, and a magick comes from them that amplifies the fairy music in lovely cello tones. The fairies project a magick that controls the colors reflected on the moving water.

"May I?" Rhydian holds his hand out to me.

"What? Dance?"

"Sure. Why let them have all the fun?"

I'm not much of a dancer, but the twinkle in his eye is challenging. "Ah . . . I make no promises—"

"About what? Dancing technique or something?"

I laugh, and so does he. I put my hand in his, and he leads me around the edge of the water in what might be a waltz. His smile lights up. The entire perimeter of the lake glows as fairies join in, contributing their magnificent colors and music. Rhydian turns me out, and I leave his hand and swing wide before I return to him. He swings me into his body.

"You're so beautiful."

My breath escapes in a shudder at being so close to him, and I find myself staring at his lips.

"May I kiss you?"

I don't answer. Instead, I pop up on my toes and connect our lips in a quick peck. He places his hand behind my neck and leans into me. His kiss is careful, teasing, and soft. A welcome sensation of electricity travels through my body straight to my toes. I kiss him back with an urgency that's returned. Wind surrounds us as if to push us closer together, and I'm lost in the moment.

Cheering pulls me from his lips. It's the fairies, and all I can do is laugh with Rhydian. "Voyeurs." Rhydian whispers.

"Apparently."

We leave the fairies, and Rhydian holds my hand the entire ride back to the manor. As the entrance gets closer, I know I'm not ready for this night to end. Still, it does. When Rhydian escorts me to the top of the manor stairs, I turn to him. "Thank you for tonight."

"Anytime. I like being with you," he laughs, and with a sly grin adds, "outside of work, that is."

"Funny."

He reaches out and tucks a strand of hair behind my ear. His hand moves slowly down my neck. I catch myself watching and stepping closer to him before he pulls me in.

"I should probably walk you in; it's late. But—"

I capture his lips with mine on the unspoken word. Our kiss deepens and our tongues tangle and explore. I'm all sensation and desire; with one hand at his neck and one on his arm, I feel like I'm spinning carefree.

Back in my room, I flop on my bed and touch my lips, reminiscing about the entire night. My magick still hums under my skin. There is no way I'm going to sleep.

My phone buzzes. A text from Rhydian.

I can't sleep. I keep thinking about kissing you.

I smile. *I was thinking the same thing.*

I know, can't get it out of my mind either.

My good mood is instantly invaded by thoughts of his blood vow, and a pit forms in my stomach. He knows my emotions. He can feel them. Heat rises to my face. I huff at the one-sided aspect of the blood vow. Nothing I feel will be unknown to him.

Willow, are you okay?

I stare at his text for a minute, my mind reeling with thoughts. Did he kiss me because he wanted to, or was he satisfying an emotional need from me? Do I want to know the real answer to that? Ugh!

Willow? Should I come over?

I hesitate. *Tired, talk to you at school tomorrow?*

Okay.

Goodnight, Rhydian.

I wait to see if he'll say anything more. He doesn't, and I immediately feel like a bitch.

Did I ruin the perfect date?

PART II

By knot of four, this power I store
By knot of five, the spell's alive

Mondays at Trinity High School are always full of weekend buzz—new gossip about hookups, breakups, and sport scores. I navigate the hallway to my locker on autopilot and spy Emily and Marco laughing. They look good next to each other, his mocha skin and white oxford shirt in complementary contrast to Emily's paleness. I wave to them and open my locker, hang my coat, and grab my books. I shove them in my backpack. I sense Rhydian's presence but don't seek him out. I can tell he's keeping his distance because of our text conversation, which has me swimming in a pool of regret.

"So, how was the date?"

"Shhh. Don't be so loud," I say to Emily.

"What's this about?" Marco asks with a smirk.

Emily fills Marco in on the date that I had with Rhydian last night.

Marco grunts. "Ah dating Rhydian, so he's around you like all the time right even here at school?"

"I guess so, why?"

"Since he's here at school now and you're a magickal royal badass, why am I being ordered by Guardians to watch over you at school?"

"What? That is not my doing, Marco, and you don't have to do it. I can certainly take care of myself," I huff.

"If only it was that easy, Willow. Did you realize I would be breaking the law if I went against Guardian orders? I mean, sure, how would they find out? We only have a couple of classes together. But if something goes down and I'm anywhere near you and don't engage, it could cost me my head or other vital parts."

Emily smacks her gum and dramatically rolls her eyes at Marco. He responds with an indignant, "What?"

"Could you be more bitchy? You're a freakin' shapeshifter, not a little puss—kitty." She winks before continuing, "Come on, tiger man, grow a pair."

"Always challenging the fighter in me. Why not the lover?"

"Gotta earn it."

"Get a room," I tease. I'm never so bold, especially in public places, to say the things they do. Heck, I'm still grappling with the fact that Rhydian can sense my emotions.

The bell rings for homeroom just in time. I can't focus on the announcements. Instead, I think about the predicament of Marco being given orders. He's ordered to do something because he goes to my school and is part of Edayri. That doesn't seem right.

It isn't as if he volunteered. Sure, I'm a little hurt that he seems put off by the idea of helping me if something happens, but in all reality, he's only my friend because I was dating Daniel. He's always been friendly to me, and he certainly flirts with Emily all the time, but we're not directly friends by ourselves.

The bell rings for first period, pulling me from my thoughts. When I arrive, Rhydian is already in his seat. He's flanked by Team Bleach Blonde with Coral at the front. He's smiling and talking with them, but his eyes are on me the moment I walk in.

"Hey, Willow."

That puts the pin in Coral, her mouth open and her perfectly manicured eyebrows creased. I smile weakly in their direction and take my seat.

During class, Rhydian looks back at me twice and catches me staring at him. He projects warmth and happiness to me through our connection. It feels intimate even though I'm surrounded by fellow students. As much as I look like I'm listening to the lecture, I'm really not. The sense that I should be in Edayri learning my duties instead of here has me doubting myself and my goals. Rhydian projects the cheering of the fairies following our kiss. I giggle and try to hide it from everyone around me. Coral notices anyway and looks from me to Rhydian.

Rhydian waits for me after class, and we leave together.

"Still need some space?" He doesn't seem angry, but his eyes are wide, waiting for my response. Goddess, I'm a brat. What am I doing? Most girls would love a guy who has an inside track on their emotions and who is sensitive to that. Here I am pouting about it like an idiot.

"No," I say. "I'm sorry. Call it a momentary over-thinking brain hiccup."

Coral approaches and I turn to Emily. Her eyes wide and mocking.

I mouth a dramatic, what? When I see Coral reach out a hand to touch Rhydian's shoulder then step into his space.

"Hey guys!" Emily interrupts, bouncing into the crowded space and hanging her arm over my shoulder. "And the sharks circle," she whispers in my ear.

"Funny," I reply.

Without a missing a beat, Coral continues. "I was curious if you'd like to get to know some of your other fellow students this weekend at my house. I'm having a little party—"

Rhydian looks at us. "Wanna go to Coral's party?" Coral's mouth drops open and I choke down a laugh as Emily announces that we will all be there.

"Oh, that's just great." Coral stares hard at Emily before focusing back on Rhydian, her smile plastered. "I'll see you then." She walks away hips swinging.

"Thanks, Coral, for the invite." Rhydian says as I elbow him.

Rhydian laughs, fidgeting with a knotted rope in his hand. "What's with the rope?"

"Oh, knot magick?" He holds it up for me to see. I raise my eyebrows. "It's almost like when girls sing that song and pull petals from a flower. It's a spell-like rhyme that we learn when we are young. 'By knot of one, the spell's begun. By knot of two, it cometh true.' You work through the knots to the end."

"So, you're wishing for something?"

"Maybe." He shrugs, watching my face, then steps closer to me.

I know how it looks to everyone around us: that we are a couple. We haven't even talked about it though. Are we dating? Sabine and Eoin mentioned Rhydian needing a cover to be with me at all times in Chepstow. Whether or not we are a couple, that would make a good cover.

Coral corners me before my organic chemistry class to ask the question I can tell she's dying to ask. "Are you and Rhydian dating?"

"I'm not sure that is any of your business, Coral."

"Cut the shit, Willow. Because if you aren't, I'm making a move."

"Yes, I think you were making a move anyway. Why does it matter what I say?"

"I'm not that person."

That's news to me, because I could have sworn that's all she ever did when I was dating Daniel. I'm tempted to search for her thoughts, which is not only wrong but also a type of magick I've never tried before. I wouldn't want to mess something up, like whatever I did to Evan. I shake my head of the idea.

Yes, you should.

"Okay, yes, we've gone out on dates and are getting to know each other. I don't think I can define it beyond that right now."

He's mine.

Coral doesn't respond; she just turns dramatically, swinging her long black hair, and walks away. Whatever. The tardy bell rings, so I step into my classroom —then freeze.

Evan is at the front of the room, horns and all for everyone to see.

"Please, have a seat. I'm your sub today. You're blocking the doorway; it's a fire hazard. Come in now please."

Marco, also apparently late, pushes me, and we enter with several other students. Marco gives me an irritated look but doesn't seem to recognize Evan. He knows Evan! Why is he acting so causal?

I look all around the classroom waiting for the cavalry, but nothing happens. Evan is talking and smiling, and on closer observation I notice a wavering of light around his body. He's projecting a different image to everyone; why can I see him as he is? I slow my breathing. If I don't control my emotions, I'll be inviting Rhydian to come into the class for sure.

The sharp elbow in my side from Marco shocks me. Evan is looking directly at me, smirking as if this is some game. "Ms. Warrington, let me ask you again: Can you advise on where you are in the chapter work?"

"Didn't Mrs. Simpson leave a lesson plan?"

"She is out unexpectedly. If you don't know, can someone else advise?"

Before anyone responds, I say, "We're on complex bonds and dissolution of materials."

"Very well, then. If everyone can go to that chapter and read for a moment, I will try to find the handout for today's sample experiment."

Marco is still staring at me, trying to figure out why I'm acting so odd. "What the hell?" he mouths. But Evan is next to our table with the missing handout that has somehow appeared.

"Are we going to have a problem, Ms. Warrington? I thought from Mrs. Simpson's note that you are her star student in this class. She said you would be willing to assist, though it seems she may be wrong."

The laughter from behind me makes the hair on my neck stand. He's trying to get a rouse from me, and at school!

"She's not wrong," I reply, staring at him hard in warning.

Marco kicks my leg. I continue to shake him off; he clearly can't see that the substitute teacher is Evan.

"We'll see. Stars are just gaseous energy that eventually combusts under changing circumstances—then, poof."

"Clearly, that's not right; that's how stars are formed under immense pressure. Is this a test?" I am trying hard not to combust myself. My classmates mirror Marco's open mouth and wide-eyed expressions. "I'm sorry, I shouldn't have—"

"Well, at least you're not tempted to be in the herd of followers." Evan waves his hand and time stops. The lights dim. "That's better."

"What the hell, Evan! Why are you here?"

"I don't have much time. We need a way to

communicate; as you say, shit is going down. Give me your hand." He rolls up his sleeve and reaches for me.

I pull from him. "No. Tell me what's going on. Here?"

He pulls my arm forward, wrapping his hand near my elbow. Reluctantly, I follow his lead so that our forearms are touching. He whispers a spell that lights up our arms, and it's as if our magick merges and flows. The lights flicker in the room.

Evan releases my arm. The real substitute teacher is standing next to me, looking confused before moving off to take his seat at Mrs. Simpson's desk.

What did I just allow Evan to do? Will Rhydian know? Marco kicks my leg. "What was that?"

"Nothing." I shake my head and pretend to read the instructions on the handout.

On the drive home, Rhydian is behind me in one of my father's flashy sports cars. He comes up on my car's tail, egging me into a chase. I grin and push the accelerator. My BMW has an engine built for speed and his comment from last week about my elderly driving fuels me. The suburban roads are not empty and they don't provide much of a challenge to getting a good lead. My car radio is blaring the bass of the radio music, which radiates through my body and charges me further. I pull into my posh neighborhood and whip into the drive that leads to the house.

The chase doesn't end there. I make my way into the house and run up the stairs to my room. Duke is at full attention when I shut my door and giggle. His entire backside shakes happily with his tail. I waggle his black ears and put my forehead to his and kiss it. The wind rushes around me as Rhydian transports into my room. Duke barks and jumps off the bed to get more head rubs from Rhydian.

"You're not supposed to transport into my room," I smirk. That was a specific order from Eoin, which means he knows Rhydian transported in the house.

"You win," he grins. "See you tonight?"

"Okay."

He reaches for my hand. Still on a high from the chase, I step up to him and lightly kiss him on the lips before stepping away with a smirk.

"Duke, wanna go outside?"

The response is a half bark and bounce. Rhydian transports out of my room. I quickly change into leggings and a T-shirt before running down the stairs with Duke at my heels. It's a race to the back door, where Duke passes me in one big jump through the doggy door and out the garage. I run pass Quinn.

"Hey, Quinn!" I yell, grabbing a frisbee out of a bin to play with Duke.

Quinn is behind me and talking to someone on his earpiece, but I have no care in the world except to play with my dog. It's been forever since we've played like this and the weather is beautiful. April in Chepstow is volatile—one minute there's snow, then the next it's sunny, warm, and cloud free like today. I wouldn't miss this opportunity for the world.

Before Duke gets too far, I shout his name. He turns to watch the frisbee fly from my hand and takes off in a big leap to catch it midair. He trots over for my praise and lets me take the frisbee back.

"One more time?" I ask as Duke waits impatiently.

I throw the frisbee in a high gentle arch. I run with him a few feet, then stand and watch him catch it again. I laugh and clap as he brings the frisbee to me. Petting his furry head, I sense a bit of vertigo, like a wave that hits and moves down my body.

I'm caught off guard as my vision wavers and changes. The dried dead grass of my yard is replaced by a bright green lawn with a technicolor effect. I shake my head but the scene in front of me stays. My legs feel like jelly and I take a moment to sit down. A man with white hair and a commanding presence appears right in front of me.

"Evan, you get back in this house right now and you apologize."

My jaw drops. It's Harkin, my grandfather; I recognize him from portraits at the manor and at the Hallowed Hall. His distinguished face and stature are the picture of legendary royalty.

A reply comes from behind me. "No. I am not apologizing to the step-monster." I turn and recognize in the small boy behind me the hair and features of my uncle. This is a young Evan.

"Don't call her that. Sabine and this family are all you have. You need to step up and take responsibility for who you are in this family."

Evan looks to be around the age of ten. He is so small and yet does not seem discouraged from talking back to Harkin, a man who towers over him and who certainly intimidates me. Evan's hands are buried deep in the pockets of his plaid shorts. He looks up at Harken. "She says I don't belong here, so how am I supposed to be part of the family? Only Nuala talks to me and cares."

Harkin ruffles Evan's wavy hair. "Come on, my boy, let's go back in the house. But you will apologize."

I watch father and son walk back toward the familiar gray stone of MacKinnon Manor. The image starts to waiver and change again, and my stomach feels it.

A voice in my head, the distinct sound of the little boy now an adult, says, "Who you are in this family? Sometimes family has the best intentions, but not ours. The legacy is poison. It seeps into the ground and affects more than us."

I respond with my thoughts to Evan. "Why show me this?"

"All the right questions; she is smart. Smart, smart, smart."

"Thank you, I guess?"

"No guessing; know it. Feel it. Observe it." Evan responds so loudly that I cover my ears. It does nothing to help.

"Geez, Evan, there is no need to yell. You realize I can hear you just fine in my head, right?"

"In your head, in my head, two heads together and two heads apart."

The rattling of Evan's thoughts in my head is starting to give me a headache. I'm not sure what he's trying to say; it's just garbled nonsense, as usual. "Esmund, Rhydian—the interlinks of the Boward lineage to the MacKinnon royalty ties. Oh, he likes your interest in Rhydian."

The view in front of me changes again, this time from the back of my house to the patio at MacKinnon Manor. I'm looking down at feet that aren't mine. My head turns toward a female voice, one I recognize. It grows more urgent. A stern sounding male voice causes me to hide behind a large group of potted plants. I peak around them toward the voices.

Esmund stands near my mother. He's reaching toward her, and she keeps backing away.

"It's over. Don't make this hard and more complicated," my mother says.

"We are betrothed, Nuala. This doesn't only affect you, it affects me and our families. This lineage was promised."

She hugs herself and takes a step forward toward Esmund. "I'm tired of being the political pawn for a royal rule that shouldn't even exist. You may want all of this power, and you may believe in its old tradition, but I'm done with it. It has made my family bitter and separated us. I want love in my life, and that's with Aiden. You may not like it, Esmund, but you need to accept it. And all I wish for you is to experience this type of love also."

I watch in awe of my mother—the boldness, the calm she possesses. Esmund's eyes look wild and he towers over her, looking like he might blow up or even hurt her. After a brief moment, his shoulders slump in total resignation.

"Nuala, I have always loved you. You minimize my experience and that wounds me."

"Esmund, you will always be a dear friend to both

myself and Aiden, but trust me when I say that you love the idea of me, not really me."

"You will regret this. Your father and mother will never accept this. My vow to you—"

"I reject your offered service of a blood vow that connects you to me."

"No!" Esmund bends forward and drops to his knee in agony.

I gasp. My mother waves her hand, and a bright white light shines from her palm like a spotlight directly on my face.

But it's not my face—it's Evan's. He was there.

There's a car in the drive, headlights fixed on my face. Duke is lying next to me. The warmth of his sun-heated fur has almost gone cold. The sky tells me that it's dusk.

"Willow? What are you doing out in the middle of the lawn? It's getting cold. You ready to come in, maybe get a bite to eat?" asks Rhydian.

I pet Duke's head and wave. "That sounds great," I shout back. I stand to walk across the lawn.

"So, there's the boy wonder. The highlight of Esmund's family. And how close you were to being siblings."

"Evan," I warn him. "How do I turn this off? You can't be in my head like this."

"Just flip the switch."

"And exactly where is the switch?"

"Oh—private time for boyfriend, eh?"

"Evan!"

"Turning the switch off, but be careful. Those

blood vows, they play havoc when they are not equal or wanted. Esmund understands this, but so far his gamble is paying off."

"I'm not something to be gambled with, Evan." I purse my lips together in an effort not to scream.

"Preach."

"Evan, you are too weird."

CHAPTER 10

Tullen is droning on about the history of Wicca in Edayri. My mind wanders to Rhydian. We're getting closer and spending a lot of time together. I'm completely attracted to him and enjoy being around him, and when he's not around I'm thinking about him. Still, the idea of the vow sits in the back of my mind.

"Earth to Willow. Earth to Will—no, wait, Edayri to Willow. Check in." I laugh and blush. "Seriously, Willow. I've been talking for over ten minutes and you're in some sort of daze. What's going on with you? Anything you say is between the two of us. Unleash it."

I cave. "Okay, here goes. What is the deal with blood vows? Because I—I really like Rhydian, but is his affection a result of his vow or by his choice?" A grin pulls at Tullen's lips, and I continue with what I'm sure is a red face. "I ask him, but he avoids the topic, and I just can't let it go. Am I stupid?"

"I see. No one doubts the connection you both have, but I see where you'd be concerned." Yes, for once some real talk. Thank you, Tullen! "Let me tie this into the history of the Goddess, the Horned God, and the beginning of Wicca."

"What? A history lesson, really?"

"The crown should be exhibiting just a little patience here, because history may help you with your current concerns."

"But I thought the Horned God was related to the birth of the demons, not Wicca. Doesn't Wicca belong with the Goddess?"

"Ah, so you are listening to me." Tullen scratches his short red scruffy beard. "Yes, it belongs to them both. The Horned God and the Goddess are responsible for Edayri. Our kind was birthed out of Edayri." Tullen pauses to make sure I'm paying attention, then continues. "The Goddess and the Horned God were connected not only by the same family but by requited love, but the Goddess also fell in love with her creations. She felt that she had built a better creation than the Almighty with doses of magick and other special abilities. The Horned God was jealous because he loved the Goddess and wanted her attention, so he gifted her with his own creation. He made a mirror of himself—you know them as demons. The Goddess took this as an insult and was outraged that he would add another creation to her beautiful, perfect world. The Horned God was offended because they are of the same family, but his difference was seen by the Goddess as a weakness and imperfect.

The bond between the Goddess and Horned God was strained. It was said the Horned God left her and the Goddess cried for weeks on end. A Wiccan by the name of Brekaen made a vow to the Goddess to honor her in a way that the Horned God could not, per his loyalty he offered to tie his soul to hers, if she would accept this he could be anything she needed. Since Brekaen was a Wiccan and part of the creation she loved, she accepted his vow, and this is where the blood vow was born. Others wanted her attention, but they were not as well-intended as Brekaen. As a result, the blood vow became one of service per serious commitment and honor, paid in blood and life. If you broke your vow, the Goddess owned your soul and the physical pain of your deceit would always be present."

"This is interesting, but what strikes me most is that you're telling me that both Wiccans and demons are from the same family? If this is true, how can Wiccans deny it?" I ask.

Tullen, ever thoughtful, pauses and scratches the side of his face where his beard and hairline meet. "It's complicated. We are full of pride, if you will, and with the love of the Goddess. Because of this, we are her perfect creations."

"We are far from perfect."

"Depends on how you define perfect. Needless to say, the Horned God felt he was giving the Goddess a gift. When she rejected it, she essentially rejected him. The result was a war between the Goddess and the Horned God and their creations, a war that has never ended. The Horned God, broken-hearted that she would choose Wiccan vows over his—a god's—turned them into enemies. Eventually the Horned God's presence faded, he no longer wanted the Goddess's acceptance."

This is the most ridiculous thing I've ever heard. Heck, in high school this is a daily occurrence—saying one thing and meaning it differently, and someone else taking offense to it. The intention behind whatever is said is not usually malicious. This is something you witness every freaking day!

I interrupt him. "Doesn't anyone get how ridiculous this is?"

"The previous ruler would not abide by that discussion, but there's certainly hope with the new ruler. An outsider." Tullen smiles.

When Rhydian first introduced me to Tullen as the historian and their moral conscience, I didn't understand, but today it is quite clear. He challenges the status quo and coveted traditions. We are alike in that regard, although I am rarely emboldened enough to act or speak. Does that make me complicit or just scared and young?

"Tullen, I am pulled in so many different directions that any type of voice I want to have is lost. I want to invoke change, but Sabine, Esmund, and others hold tradition in their fist and almost beat me with it. As you said, I'm an outsider, and I'm certainly being treated like one. I want to be here, but I don't fit, and that makes me not want to be here. I fit in Chepstow—or I guess I used to. My life is at a fork in the road, literally." I put my face in my hands and breathe.

Tullen is leaning forward, his elbows on his knees, hands clasped, listening. "I can't imagine. I would think that part of you is screaming to get out. Willow, don't let that part take a backseat, because at some point it will consume you and you might do something you regret. Just because something has always been one way doesn't mean it is the right or the only way." He watches me carefully. "Form your own opinions. Be aware of them. I love my Wiccan heritage and who I am, but because of the system we live in, I have had a very different upbringing and outlook than others who live here. Take Thaxam, for instance. He's a demon who certainly has a different take on Edayri."

"Tullen, are the Emissaries just a group opposing Wiccan dominance and rule? Are there any Wiccans who are part of it?"

"The Wiccans may not show it, but most lower covens are part of the Emissaries, or at minimum agree that all beings should be equal. You come from a world that has fought for equality across the Terra realm. Here, no one challenges the Wiccan royal rule with any great success. But like I said, there's hope."

I sag in my seat, and Tullen stands and claps my knee.

"I'm here to talk anytime you need, Willow. I believe Cross is waiting for you; it might be the perfect time to reflect. Training is always a good way to take out the frustrations and bothersome questions that plague your brain."

I change clothes in the training room and stop in front of the mirror. My hair is dark brown now, like my fathers, and my facial features are like my mothers, yet I am uniquely me. Judgment seems to stare back at me. What can I do? I'm quite small and I'm not fearless.

Yet you are powerful.

My magick flows on my skin instantly. I didn't call it, but it flows, and the crown appears on my forehead and lifts high like a hologram.

So, I'm powerful. Sure. What do I do with it?

Anything.

And that's what scares me.

"Hey, ya ready?" Cross is bouncing around on the mat, sweat starting to bead on his forehead. I nod back at him. "Let's get started then." He has me run on the treadmill for five minutes, then he has me limber up before we get into physical rounds of offense and defense training.

"Not that I'm complaining, but damn, yer quiet. Are ya not talkin' because ya want to quiet the mind, or is this mind to loud for ya?"

"Right, you complaining? No, never." I say, then blink dramatically.

"All right then." He puts on a padded vest that fits his blocky muscular build snuggly. "Let's see which it is. Attack, and no magick. Show me!"

"No magick?" I bring it up on my forearms and watch the swirls extend to my fingers. "Why not? Afraid?"

"Hells, I should be, but nah. If ya got none, then

what? Stop testing my good nature and come at me!"

Part of me wants to knock his smug face across the room with a light blast from my hands. The other part—the competitive part—wins. I run up with my sparring gloves and move through the drill attack combo—left, right, left, high knee to round kick. He's blocking me and meeting me at every turn. I hit harder and faster, landing a few good ones that Cross shrugs off easily. The physical combat is becoming second nature. I focus on the movements.

"AHH!" I yell, my movements a blur.

Cross is no longer in defense but attacking me, and I easily maneuver around him. I'm in control. The scared girl from the attack in the alley all that time ago, the same girl who ran through the woods after meeting her first demon, is gone.

There is a loud, slow clap from the side of the gym.

We stop fighting. Cross smiles and waves someone in. It is Tullen. I try to catch my breath.

"She's still holding back," Cross says, and that shocks me. My magick flares at him. "Come on, ya are. Yer speed and efforts are not from the middle."

"Boy, I can't wait to witness you knock Cross on his ass." Tullen smiles and grabs a bo staff from the wall. "I was quite sure that today might have been that day."

"Aye, so tis to quiet yer head then." Cross tosses me a towel and I wipe the sweat from my face and neck.

"Yeh, I guess," I respond.

"She's struggling with the history and duty of royal rule," Tullen announces as he tosses a staff to Cross. They circle each other, and Tullen twirls his side to side in big sweeps, approaching Cross.

Cross's twirl overhead is less theatrical, and before I know it, they are smacking staffs and sweeping each other in a fight. They both anticipate each other's moves. They smile, taunting each other. It's a ballet I like to watch.

Tullen is flat on his back with Cross's staff on his chest before he taps the mat.

"There, the answer is no—again," Cross says, exasperated.

I wonder what the question was, but Tullen seems content.

"Willow, ya need to show them who wears the crown. The crown doesn't wear ya." Cross points to me before hanging the bo staff up on the wall. "Ya do that, and ya give hope to the masses as ya did in disbanding the high council."

This is the reason Cross tolerates me. Change.

"How is that?" I ask.

"Cause when battles are unjust to the innocent, they also tear the fabric of those who serve." Cross stares at me while he speaks. "My parents died serving the royal crown, but because we are from a lower coven, it isn't considered a significant loss."

"I'm sorry, Cross. I would never—"

"I get that."

This whole cast and the royal system is messed up, and now I am the head of it.

CHAPTER 11

After my shower, I stretch my neck, close my eyes, and breathe slowly. My muscles are sore from the workout with Cross. I lay down on the small sofa next to Duke in our sitting room. Then, out of nowhere, the vertigo. My vision flickers. I blink and observe that I'm no longer on the sofa; I'm sitting on a small cot in a medical tent. Blurs of people and demons walk by, attending to the injured.

A laugh bursts through my lips, catching me off guard because it isn't my voice. The hands I hold out in front of me are strong and thick, black, blue, and stained with blood.

Why are you happy?

A woman comes into view—no one I recognize. She has kind, dark eyes that seemed oddly familiar. "Oh, Evan, what happened?"

"I'm ready. I miss her so much. It would not be a bad thing to join her." The woman is moving things at the head of the cot. She takes a stethoscope and listens to my chest—Evan's chest.

"Who do you miss, Evan?"

The name lifts off my lips in a breathy declaration. "Meghan." My eyes shut and I see her—the full face and wide eyes, the dark chocolate, thick hair that curls at her waist. She is curvy and short, and her smile melts my heart. For me and only me. Her unconditional love, her quick wit, her brazen attitude.

My eyes—our eyes—are shocked by the penlight the woman shines. We focus and hoarsely call out, "Meghan?" We reach for her wrist, but her touch on our face is not Meghan's small hand. Her eyes are not the wide, deep purple we love.

"Can you tell me where you are?"

We don't want to. Our voice catches in our throat; we shut our eyes. The pain pounds in our head. Tears cloud our eyes.

"The Emissaries camp. MacKinnon Manor—"

"Evan, you're going to be just fine." The woman says some type of enchantment over us and our legs straighten, our arms relax, and we drift to lay down prone on the cot. "You've got more work to do. It is not your time, Evan."

We remember the venom of our words. "I did a bad thing. Willow—I couldn't save Aiden. Abby, she hurts—it won't be mended. It will be worse. She's not ready."

The woman, Abby, yells something behind her, and a young boy brings her a glass tube with a glowing amber liquid.

She gently pulls our chin down, and we comply. The liquid is warm and slides down our throat. "This will take away the physical curse, but the mental one, I'm afraid, is one we'll have to examine later."

We look at our hands; the black and blue starts to fade and return to their natural skin color. "She's going into the lion's den."

"Well, according to my brother, she's quite the lion herself. She'll need that spunk against my father. Drift, Evan, into a healing sleep." Abby's words echo in our ears.

"They will break her—"

"Shhh. Drift, Evan. Remember, the lioness is the bravest of the pride. She is a lot like Nuala and her father. She will recognize the hypocrisy."

"Compulsions, vows, the loss of free will. They will steal it from her, may even kill it out of her. I did a bad thing, an awful thing." Our chest feels heavier with each word and a fog comes over us, pushing us into the cot.

Abby caresses our face, her touch comforting.

My eyes—our eyes—are heavy. The image flutters, my heart picks up, joy replaces my guilt. My soul returns to my body.

I suck in air abruptly, pushing myself up to stand. I'm back in my suite at MacKinnon Manor.

"Oh, Goddess." I massage my throat and feel the ache of my bones. I wish there was some sort of warning before I experienced Evan's memories. I can't breathe. I walk around the sitting area and open the doors to the outside. The cooling wind greets me and takes away the weight of Evan's sadness and heartache.

"He tried to help," I say to the stars above.

Knock.

"Yes?"

"Lady MacKinnon would like your company for the evening meal in the dining hall in a half hour."

⚜

Entering the dining hall, I find my seat at the end of the table where two place settings are stationed. The white and gold plates shine from the light of the crystal chandelier overhead. Sabine sweeps into the room. I stand before she quickly waves me to sit.

"Although we do a lot of crown business here, this is your family home too. Let's relax tonight."

We engage in small discussions, and things are pleasant. Then I ask her about my grandfather, the Wiccan King.

Sabine's eyes light up and crinkle at the corners. "Harkin was a difficult man, very stubborn at times, but so easy on the eyes." I smile. "I knew him in my younger years but never paid him much attention because our family lines and covens were not intertwined. We were betrothed, per custom. I could love and hate that man all in one breath. But I think that's how most marriages go. I do miss him, though."

This is a side of Sabine I never anticipated. Her relaxed demeanor and personal engagement with me while discussing her husband are something new.

"You sound fortunate to have fallen in love."

"It's certainly something we need to discuss for you as well."

"What, discuss me falling in love?" I stammer.

"Discuss the traditions of royal betrothals and linages of noble covens."

"I don't want that." I look away before I continue. "I'm having a hard enough time understanding blood vows and why Rhydian seems so happy about it. I don't want to get married unless I'm in a relationship with someone I love, and even then, only if it is the next step for us in our lives. Besides, I'm too young."

Sabine sits back in her chair and lifts wine to her mouth. "Yes, it's time some things change. I don't disagree."

My shoulders relax. Evan holds grudges against Sabine from when he was a little boy. Sabine's protectiveness and support of me show me something else entirely from Evan's experience. I wonder if I can share this with him the way he shares his experiences with me.

"But, darling, some things need to remain in tradition too, or they get lost to future generations. I see so much of Nuala and Aiden in you. You know, Nuala and Aiden were a perfect match, balancing light and dark so perfectly. If things had been different in their matching . . . well, it would have been a different life for all."

I'm surprised by her comment that they were a perfect match. Knowing the answer, I ask a question that will test my theory.

"Were they betrothed?"

Her eyes come back to me from wherever her thoughts had taken her. "No, they were not. She was promised in betrothal to Esmund, actually. They all grew up together and were in the same friend groups. It was hard on Esmund when she chose Aiden and they married, but over time the friendships repaired and remained."

I lean back in my chair and feel more at ease. Did I think she would lie to me? No. She seems more flexible than what Evan tells me.

"The bond your parents held was so strong. Stronger than any vow. It was you, Willow. You brought so much to them without even being born yet, only conceived. The promise of you gave them freedom, a linage."

It's a lovely moment of closeness that I have never felt before with Sabine. Feeling like I'm in a safe space, I jump in the deep end.

"Do you support change? I mean, Wiccan and Edayri change?"

I wait as she takes another drink of her wine.

"Willow, times are changing, but you have to measure how that change will affect everyone. I am one for tradition, but I also know those of us left are older and it is time for a new regime."

"But if the majority of Edayri want this change, then why stay stuck? There is more to Edayri, and I've only seen a small fraction of it."

The relaxed aspect of the room changes; there's a

shift in the air. I sense someone in the doorway behind me. Sabine's face becomes hard, her lips pushed together. "Don't disappoint your parent's legacy or this family, Willow. Your every action and reaction is measured." She stands, redirecting her attention with a charming smile. "Hello, Esmund. Won't you come in?"

I turn to watch Mr. Boward enter.

"Pardon the intrusion, but you wanted the report. I'm happy to advise that I have been appointed in the official capacity of bridge to the Wiccan communities with the support of the noble coven, in addition to my current role as royal Scepter to you, of course."

"You've done well for yourself, Esmund." Sabine smiles but it doesn't reach her eyes. She is putting on her political face for him.

I stand and walk to the doorway near Mr. Boward. "I'm going to my room. Thank you, Sabine, for dinner and our talk."

"Anytime. Let us continue our discussion soon, Willow."

We will, I'm sure of it.

"Good evening, Willow." Mr. Boward squints his eyes and looks down his nose at me. "I understand you will not be here through the weekend. Going back to the Chepstow so soon?"

"Well, I'm returning for tonight. Can you request a royal Guardian as an escort? Will that make it better?"

Mr. Boward's sly grin reminds me of the devil. I want to smack the demur grin off Esmund's face. He has planned no less for me and Rhydian. I wonder if Rhydian is even aware of what his father's plans are. I'm not fond of the matchmaker grins across his and Sabine's faces.

They aren't wrong, granted—I'm totally falling for Rhydian—but this is frustrating beyond belief.

CHAPTER 12

Rhydian and I transport into the foyer of my home holding each other's hands. Finally, away from duty, I lean in and gaze up into his eyes. Someone clears their throat from the side of the staircase. Rhydian is the first to release his hand. I turn to find Eoin with a sandwich in hand, dressed in jeans and a sweater. His eyes look tired.

"Returning early? I thought you were due back tomorrow?" There is slamming in the kitchen. "Quinn is cleaning up."

Rhydian stands tall in front of Eoin, his commander, and says, "We've been invited to attend a party tonight that a school friend is hosting. Would it be acceptable, and beneficial to our cover at school, for us to attend this party?"

A lot of students will be at Coral's party, including all my friends.

Eoin is looking at me, eyebrow high. I shrug, trying to look like I care just enough but not too much. "It could be a good thing to go to some of my normal activities outside of school. It would be suspicious if I didn't. And," I throw in, "I would love to just hang with my friends for a night."

Eoin takes a bite of his sandwich, chews, and swallows before he speaks, watching both of us closely. "Both of you together, the entire time within eyesight." Why am I blushing? He meant for security only. "Do you both understand?"

We both answer quickly with a yes, Rhydian's more formal by adding a "sir." Eoin proceeds up the stairs and leaves us in the foyer. I spy Quinn at the top of the stairs. Didn't Eoin say he was in the kitchen? Strange. He quickly waves to me before rounding the corner out of sight.

"Should we leave now? The party is well underway."

Surveying myself, I realize I don't need to change —my chucks, dark jeans, and sweater are exactly what I would wear to Coral's anyway. "Yes, just let me grab my coat. Will we transport or drive over?"

"We'd be less conspicuous if we drove."

Silly of me to think differently; of course, we will drive to Coral's house together. I'm getting used to transporting magickly. With my coat in hand, I pet Duke goodbye and meet Rhydian in the garage. I get behind the wheel of my BMW. He has a wide grin on his face.

"What is so entertaining?" I ask, backing out of the garage.

"Nothing. I'm just happy to leave the confines of

the walls that keep you hidden, not unlike the night at the lake with the fairies."

He's right—it's freedom on another level, and another date night. This is more public though. My classmates will see us together, and somehow that makes me nervous. It's been just us and our private moments, although I guess the fairies at the lake make it not so private.

"Are you ready for us to be public?" he asks.

I'm surprised at his question. Is he insecure about us?

Be bold.

"Rhydian, are we more than . . . tied in vows? Are we dating?"

The choke of air startles me. He lays his hand on mine, covering the gear shift. The Guardian wrist cuff is cold to the touch. "I don't think dating is more than tied in vows. Simply, I like you, Willow, and I would like more romantic opportunities. If that is dating, then yes. I don't want you with anyone else."

He sounds so formal and yet natural at the same time. I'm awkward. Heat rises on my face and I keep my eyes on the road.

"Are my intentions not clear to you?" he asks.

I turn into Coral's neighborhood and enter the gate code to gain entry. Her neighborhood is a high-end cluster of houses with manicured lawns, carefully placed trees, and intentional landscaping. I turn and see Rhydian staring at me with a smile. I fumble with my car and drive forward through the gate. "Yes, I just—I feel like I have more choice than you, and I don't want to influence your feelings or—I just—okay, I'm embarrassed for even asking now."

"Don't be. I—how do I say this without scaring you off the road?"

The hair on the back of my neck tingles, and I shift in my seat. I breathe steadily, waiting for a full minute before he says, "The vow is one of duty, but my heart is another matter, and it is mine, Willow."

He says my name like a lyric, and my chest pounds in my ears. I pull over behind a line of cars parked in front of Coral's long drive and turn to him, turning off the car. His are eyes watching my every move, traveling to my lips and settling on my eyes. How can I doubt the way he feels?

"Um—

"I know, we'll take this slow, but you want to explore this too."

Boy, I do. Why does it scare me?

"Talk to me, Willow."

Is he nervous? His eyes wander around my face as if he's mapping it to recall later. His mouth opens slightly, and he takes a shallow breath. He's waiting and wanting. I lean across the console that divides us and kiss him.

I touch his smooth face with my hand and my lips tentatively move his. I open my eyes and start to pull back, but his eyes are closed, and he's kissing me back. The warmth and excitement urge us on, and we open to each other, our tongues entangled in a slow, sweet dance. I pull back from him, grinning.

"We are dating then," Rhydian says, grinning in a cocky manner.

"Yes, we are," I respond.

We both leave the car and arrive hand in hand at Coral's party.

A weight is lifted off my shoulders, and I lean into Rhydian, not caring to hide my smile. I'm with Rhydian and my friends, and everything is normal.

Everyone is in the backyard. Emily spots us and immediately makes a scene by pointing to our hands. "So—?"

"Yeah," I say.

Emily hands us both cups with drinks. "Adorable blushing. It's time to celebrate!"

Lucy and Daniel approach us smiling. Lucy mouths the word "nice" when she sees Rhydian and I hand in hand. She leans into Daniel and kisses him on the cheek. I smile easily. We are all moving forward.

The party is a full-on rage. I let down my hair and have fun with Emily and our friends. We dance on top of the pool's hard cover. I feel the buzz of the drinks and swing my hips and long hair to the music. Emily and Marco are breakdancing, of all things, to head-banging music. We're all laughing and smiling. As the music changes, Marco turns me in a twirl, his dance style the opposite of what everyone else is doing.

Rhydian is laughing and talking to the football team. He watches me, smiling. He is so good looking, almost unreal, and he's dating me. His eyes travel over my body, and I slow my sway and crook my finger to lure him toward me. He strides toward me and puts his hands on my waist, then leans down into my neck, where he kisses me just below the ear. Everyone is fading around us—the music, the laughter—

A sudden burst of wind bellows through the party, carrying a dark shadowy figure and a shriek that rings in my ears. Lucy comes running, screaming, into the group. She is heading straight for me.

Instinct and training kick in before I can think, and I duck and throw a light ball at the shadowy figure. The figure dodges it, undisturbed by the action. I stumble on my feet before Rhydian taps his wrist cuff and is in full armor. He puts himself between us. The air around me crackles like a storm has been summoned, lightning gathering and popping across the sky. I can't track the action but see Rhydian's arm swing down with his blade. Lucy screams as if she were injured. The shadowy figure disappears from sight. My eyes find Emily, who watches Lucy fall but doesn't move from holding her staff to the ground. I realize that the students are stunned in place, frozen to their spots by Emily. Marco hollers and walks a limping Daniel toward the group.

"Shit, what was that?" Daniel says, looking around in horror at the students frozen in place. His eyes grow wider, his mouth parting, when he spots Emily radiating magick from her staff freezing who she can lay her eyes on. "What is going on?" Lucy runs into his arms, hugging him and quietly sobbing.

"It's a valkyrie phantom, but I don't know how it would have entered the Terra realm," Emily says.

"Are you sure?" Rhydian asks, his brows knit together. "I've never seen one. I thought that once the Norse realm collapsed—"

Emily purses her lips and stares down Rhydian. The silence is deafening.

"Damn." Marco says, breaking the silence. "Valkyrie?"

Daniel is stone-like, expressionless, just watching us. Watching me. He is eerily calm as he stares and pulls Lucy in closer. She seems oblivious. Before I can say anything, Rhydian is in front of me.

"It's gone, but—um, your crown is high and bright, Willow."

Shit. My magick is flowing all over me.

"It's all lies, isn't it?" Lucy sobs.

"Lucy . . ." Emily warns, but she keeps going.

"Wiccan. Is that it, Willow? Looks a bit more than some religion. How could you not say anything to me? We're best friends!"

"I didn't say anything for your protection—for both you and Daniel." Her eyes are haunted and sad. I brush my hand through my hair and turn to Emily. "When did you tell her?"

"Don't speak as if I'm not here! And it was a week ago," Lucy snaps. She's pulled back from Daniel and is hugging herself.

"Willow, I've got to call this in," Rhydian says.

Daniel's face is suddenly open, and his eyes are searching my face. "I knew this, didn't I?"

I nod to Daniel, realizing that the magick that locked his memory is breaking. He's going to remember the attack at my house. Removing that memory will have been for nothing now. My heart breaks at the turn of his head, as if he's reading my mind.

Eoin transports in next to Rhydian and me. He's looking me over and directing the three Guardians who came with him. Emily, still holding the staff, begins to shake.

"Hey guys, this is starting to get a bit tough—holding time in place for all these people. How about you all transport out and Marco and I will cause a distraction to confuse everyone into what they think they saw."

Eoin agrees and directs everyone but Marco and Emily transport. Lucy and Daniel are transported by Quinn and Tullen to my house. Rhydian and I join hands and wait to transport since everyone saw us in this spot. Eoin and the other Guardians are at posts to ensure everything goes smoothly.

So much for the buzz I was sporting earlier. Rhydian studies me carefully. I almost miss Emily releasing her staff. Marco, covered in a black sheet, rushes through the crowd of students yelling. Everyone seems confused until he tackles Emily to the ground, laughing, rolling around, and kissing. Everyone seems to buy it, but I spy Coral in the window of her room looking out. She knows something is up. Rhydian and I make our way to leave the party, and he hands the keys to a Guardian to drive the car home.

We slip into a dark shadow.

"I'm sorry about—"

His finger is on my lips. "Don't be sorry. Some things are out of our control." Before I can respond, he gently kisses me, and we are transporting. It's a wild sensation the closeness of us, how we meld together. The push and pull I expect is barely noticeable with the force of our bodies together. Maybe I'm still feeling the effects of the alcohol? As the world fades around us, I wonder, can we stay like this and not return to my house? The reality is, I don't want to stop kissing him. We move in the flow of magick; it's peaceful and wraps us together like a warm blanket. My feet don't touch the ground.

Only when we pull from our kiss do we hear the loud yelling.

CHAPTER 13

Tullen and Quinn, standing to the side, shrug when they see Rhydian and me. Lucy and Daniel stop yelling and go in different directions in my house, Daniel into the sitting room and Lucy back toward the kitchen.

I feel a pang of guilt. "I need to talk with Daniel." Rhydian's face is unreadable. "Are you okay?"

Rhydian's hand drops to my waist to pull me closer. "Yea. I'm trying not to be the jealous type."

"There is no reason to be. Daniel and I are friends. We have history, and I need to explain."

"I get it. I'm going to check in with Eoin and get an update on status. I'll be back in the office." He leans down and kisses me one last time.

Tullen follows Rhydian while Quinn nods and goes back toward the kitchen. Daniel is pacing in the sitting room, chewing the side of his cheek.

"Daniel?"

He doesn't stop pacing. "When? This was before your Dad, wasn't it?"

I step in front of him. "Yes. You got hurt and I couldn't see any way for us to be together, so we broke up."

"No, we didn't. You lied to me by changing my memory. Willow, why?" He turns away from me, his voice getting louder. "Don't answer that. I know—you were trying to protect me!" Throwing up his hands, he sits in a chair. I take the one across from him.

"I'm sorry, Daniel, I really am. I did have the best intentions. I thought it would be best, considering you were hurt right here at my house. And when I say hurt, Daniel, you almost died. Right there." I point down the hallway toward the staircase.

His eyes land on the staircase, and he stares for a moment. "You chose someone else, too."

"Rhydian? That's a recent development."

"Maybe for you, but I remember everything. He healed me, but he did it for you, not out of the goodness of his heart. You just threw us away and took my choices away. Talk about a passive aggressive breakup."

"Dan—

"Seriously? You took away my choices and what we were together. God, Willow! Did I mean that little to you? How fucked up is it that you pushed me toward Lucy, your best friend. You've mourned our breakup, but for me, this is fresh." He stands, the chair moving with force as he turns back to pace in front of the window. His shoulders are square on his lean, muscular frame, his blond hair messy from constantly running his hand through it.

"Daniel. Please look at me." When he turns, my stomach twists. "I'm truly sorry. What I did was horrible. I know how it feels to have your choices taken from you, and I can't believe I did that to you, regardless of my intentions. I don't want you in this crazy magickal world. It's dangerous. My father, Mrs. Scott —" My voice hitches at their names and tears threaten to fall. "Daniel, I can't lose my friends as a result of who I am. It would break me."

"I understand, but I'm pissed about it." His shoulders relax. "It's like all my closest friends are in this secret club, and I'm looking through the window. Lucy has been lying to me for over a week and pushing our relationship. I just don't know anymore, about anything. And Marco—well, he let me in on it a long time ago, actually, but not . . ."

So, Marco confided in Daniel, sharing who and what he is? He trusted Daniel and gave him a choice. Marco is the smart one among us.

I finish his thought out loud. "The same."

"Yeah."

"In my defense, he's had more time to be used to what he is. I learned at the start of the school year."

Daniel laughs almost mocking. "And from what I hear you're the Queen? And have some serious powers."

"Yeah, something like that." I try to grin back. "Listen, this world is only expanding for me and sounds like it will for Lucy too. You'll need to really consider what you want for your life, Daniel. No warnings or opinions from my side." I hold up my hands in surrender.

He pulls me into a hug. It's nice, but different— not like the closeness we had before. Our history connects us. Goddess, I miss him. He was my first love. "I'm going to check on Lucy. Do you want to come?" Daniel declines, saying he needs space.

Lucy is crying when I find her. Quinn is near the refrigerator, staring at the floor with his hands in his pockets.

"Lucy?" I grab a napkin and sit next to her in the breakfast nook.

"Are you going to take Daniel back now?"

"No, no. Why would you even think that? Listen, it isn't like that anymore. I should have been a better friend to you, Lucy. I've been all over the place and I should have been more open about everything."

"Daniel is so angry with me. Hell, I'm angry."

I hug her around her small shoulders. "I'm sorry, Lucy. I really am."

"Tell me then."

Sitting at the table, I tell Lucy about my vast Wiccan heritage, the throne, my grandmother, and how I accepted the crown and am now the Wiccan Queen in Edayri. She doesn't ask any questions, just listens intently. I tell her about how she was abducted with my father and how Emily and I found and rescued her. Her face softens, and one stray tear falls down her cheek.

She doesn't remember any of it. It's as if I'm telling

her a story of fiction, except now that Emily has revealed her heritage and she's seen the phantom attack, she has no doubts.

"I haven't been honest with you, Willow. I have a confession too. I've always been jealous of you and Daniel. I've had a crush on him since he and I were in elementary school. When he asked me to prom, I knew it was as friends because he had asked you first and you said no."

Watching her, I realize that she's bottled this up for a long time. Didn't I always realize she had a crush on him? Was I selfish in dating him in front of her? "You never said anything. You even encouraged me to date him, junior year."

"I wanted the best for you both then, and, well, now I just—I don't want you and him together. I'm in love with him, Willow."

I'm not sure how to respond to the torment in my best friend's eyes. "Lucy, it is in the past. Let's just move forward. There is no ill will at all, truthfully."

We hug.

"Well, can I join in?" Emily asks.

Lucy's back straightens. She stands and leaves, silently walking past Emily. Emily and I follow her into the foyer.

Eoin, Cross, and Rhydian are in the foyer with Daniel and Marco.

"Can you give me a ride home?" Lucy asks Marco and Daniel.

"Sure."

"Lucy, you can't avoid me, or this." Emily reveals

herself in her valkyrie warrior mode, complete with brass armor and eagle headdress. She produces her fighting staff and hits the floor with it. The echo rumbles in the silence.

"You have to accept this, Lucy."

Lucy looks away from Emily, her jaw locked, and walks outside. Daniel follows her.

Marco looks at Eoin. "Being compelled by Wiccan rule takes away a bit of my free will. Can I leave?"

"Do you have any additional intel?" Eoin asks.

Marco tells Eoin that the phantoms have been conjured by very powerful Wiccans. He warns that someone is toying with Lucy and most likely with me, but he doesn't have a clue who it is. Clearly, they are tracking us somehow or they wouldn't have known our location at the party.

"Thank you, Marco," Eoin says. He turns to Rhydian and the other Guardians to give orders about perimeter sweeps and guard schedules.

Marco rolls his eyes behind Eoin's back. I can't stand that my friend is being forced into watching and reporting, or that he's being treated like a second-class citizen because he's not a Wiccan.

Wear the crown.

"Marco," I call out. He stops and I approach him. "I'm done with compulsion. Marco, I release you from the compelling order." I touch his shoulder, instructing my word and magick to undo whatever was cast on him to obey orders. I concentrate, allowing my magick to guide me. A dull light enters my fingertips, as if pulling the magick off him. It is working.

Eoin's face is stone and unmoving, but his eyes say he isn't happy with me. I don't care; the smile on Marco's is the only one I'm looking for. It gives me satisfaction.

"Thank you, Willow. I would have helped you anyway." He leans to the side to eye Eoin. "Because we are friends." He turns to go, closing the front door behind him as he joins Daniel and Lucy on the front lawn.

Turning back to the foyer, I see that Cross is grinning with Emily. Rhydian is smirking, but Eoin is unmoving.

CHAPTER 14

Emily stays over at my house without asking, which makes me smile. She's already shed her warrior valkyrie armor for the clothing she was wearing before. I wonder if she has something like the wrist cuff the Guardians wear to retract her armor. She looks tired from the long evening.

Emily makes her way upstairs. When I go to follow, Rhydian reaches for my hand.

"Can we talk for just a second?"

Eoin and Tullen are making their way back toward my father's office.

"Sure. Emily, I'll be up in just a few minutes."

"Don't take too long. I will not be responsible for the mess that may ensue." She laughs as she takes the stairs two at a time.

Just when she's out of sight, Rhydian sits down on the stairs. "So, I sort of eavesdropped on your conversation with Daniel."

Okay . . . That's interesting. I don't think I said

anything that he wouldn't expect, but now I'm starting to get a little nervous.

He clasps his hands together, almost wringing them. "You had a powerful connection with Daniel—"

I put my hand on his and stare into his eyes. "Rhydian. I didn't go about things the right way with Daniel, and I needed to apologize to him. That doesn't change anything between Daniel and me. We will always have a past and an affection for each other. He was my first love, but you—it doesn't change how I feel about you. I just want to make sure it is a personal choice."

"Why wouldn't this be our choice? I don't want to be the only party who's feeling this way."

I watch his handsome face, the way his eyes are cast down. His confidence seems to have gone.

"It's been a long night," I say. "Maybe we can talk about this more tomorrow? Maybe go on another date?" His lips quirk to the side. I push his arm, trying to lighten the mood.

"Absolutely. Although I anticipate Eoin's going to restrict your travel, so maybe we can have a night in. Watch a movie?"

"That sounds perfect." I kiss him lightly on the lips before I run up the stairs with a pep in my step. Opening my bedroom door, I find Emily sprawled on my bed and Duke lying next to her in full snuggle mode.

"Girl, you cannot have my dog. Duke, what are you doing?"

Duke jumps up, and this has Emily clutching her

stomach as she rolls away in laughter. Duke bounds over to me his whole backside wagging in happiness. My mood immediately elevates. I waggle his ears before he darts out my bedroom door.

"So, do tell. I want all the deets on Rhy and you." Emily moves over and I plop next to her.

"I really like him, but this whole blood vow thing . . . He's, like, proud about the vow, and half the time I'm just embarrassed that he can sense my emotions. I'm trying—"

"And you feel guilty. Like you're taking advantage or something?"

I close my eyes because, yeah, if I can do things with my magick just by thinking about it, how do I know?

"Get over yourself a little, Will. If he says he likes you, let it be as simple as that. Don't overcomplicate. My motto: love who loves you back, end of the story."

"Oh, what a motto. Is this an equal opportunity for Cross and Marco too?" I laugh and throw a small pillow at her. She smiles, her eyes glinting.

Emily stands on the bed and, in dramatic fashion, falls on her back and yells, "I can't help it! They are both so delectable in different ways. What's a girl to do?"

"Ah. According to you, love who loves you back." I smash her with my bigger pillow. She grabs and hugs it.

"Exactly. And see how happy I am?"

We start throwing my stuffed animals and laughing so hard I can't stop. Emily blares the music, and before I know it, we are dancing and jumping on my bed like we are twelve. Maybe she is right to live for the moment and keep things simple. Duke bounces around my room, knocking my cell phone off its charger.

I jump down from the bed. Picking up my phone, I notice that Lucy has texted me.

Please tell Emily to give me some space.

"What is it?" Emily asks.

"Lucy. What is going on? Why is she so angry at you specifically? I mean, it's all crazy town, but one minute she doesn't want exclusion, then when we open up she does?"

"She is not handling this as well as you did. Lucy is headstrong and good at playing victim, not unlike my sister, her mother."

"Wow. Well, it is a little trippy that you're her aunt, Em. Come on. You guys were friends and hanging before I even moved here."

"Yeah." Emily's breath hitches. "I was never quite sure if she would present valkyrie traits. Honestly, I figured if it didn't happen by her sixteenth birthday, it wouldn't. But then your magick was unbound, and magick in this realm was happening, and I thought, heck, she could be a late bloomer."

"So, what happened that landed you in the Terra realm?"

Emily seems far off in thought before she speaks. "My family stayed to get everyone to Edayri safely during the Norse realm collapse. My sister gave Lucy to her father. She would have most likely raised Lucy in Edayri, but my father demanded Freya stay in the Norse realm. I promised to watch over Lucy." She shrugs and smiles.

Her story doesn't make complete sense, but she's too quiet, so I ask, "Inquiring minds want to know—how old are you?"

She smiles extra wide before saying, "A shocking seventeen years old for about seven hundred years—but only the last seventeen here, of course."

I whistle in shock, which has Emily laughing even more. "Impressive, right? I'm so down with the adulting of life but refuse to be one."

☙❧

When did I fall asleep? Emily and I stayed up talking about everything and nothing all at once, and it was glorious. Emily's snoring, on the other hand, is anything but pleasant. As I blindly pet Duke, my mind wanders.

Happy that I released Marco from the spell that was forced on him, I think about Rhydian. Can I release him from his blood vow? Would he be as happy as Marco? I doubt it; he says it's an honor. I can't help but think about how we'd be without the vow. Would he still have as much interest in me? Is there something that attracts me to him as a result of the vow? I shake my head. The man is well beyond attractive, so no, I'd still be drawn to him. But it's not just his appearance anymore. It's the way he teases and laughs with me; how he touches me and holds me.

He knows when to back off so I can think without pressure.

I'm going to go crazy mulling this over. I'm totally overthinking it all. I slip out of bed and go down the back stairs to the kitchen, following a delicious smell.

Eoin in the kitchen. I look at the clock. It's 5 a.m.

"Wow. Early riser, huh?"

Eoin turns his head from the gas stove and smiles. "That or insomniac, but let's go with early riser. Want a veggie omelet?" He tosses the folded egg in the pan and grabs the plate next to him. In a single fluid movement, the omelet is on the bar in front of me.

"Thank you. This is amazing," I mumble through the first hot bite in my mouth.

Eoin whisks the egg mixture and starts cooking the next masterpiece on the stove. He does have a skill in the kitchen.

"What's on your mind?" he asks.

It's a simple question, but I don't want to share about Rhydian. It's awkward since Rhydian is under his command. Eoin feels like a parent figure to me, and he's a straight shooter. My parents come to mind, then my connection to Evan and the memories he keeps showing me of his life as a MacKinnon.

"Evan, huh?"

"What, can you read minds now?" I almost choke.

He pats my back. "No, it's what I've been thinking about. Just a good guess. We haven't fully talked about it still—the abduction and Evan." Eoin raises an eyebrow at me and waits for me to talk.

"The kids who abducted me did so because they

wanted me to reverse the magick that I cursed Evan with when we fought those months back, when my father died. And I guess I did curse him, although it's not clear to me how . . . But Evan says it's a gift." I shrug my shoulders.

Eoin is calmly finishing the last bites of his omelet, so I continue. "There are so many different sides to every story. I don't know which side I'm on and where I fit into the grander scheme. I thought I wanted my old life—what I've been calling normalcy—but every time I try, I'm thrown into the complete opposite. But being the Wiccan Queen fits. And that scares me. And I think my mother and father felt the same way, and Evan seems to be directing me toward that too. I'm afraid because . . . what I've always wanted will be gone."

I exhale the words sharply. My eyes sting. This is the piece that I've had yet to say to myself—the reality that "normal" is teetering on a high wire. The more I walk, the less likely I can turn around to go back to my life before.

"That's a lot to grapple with. There is certainly a lot of pressure on you, Willow. But I promise you, I am here for you. Not Sabine or the noble covens—just you."

The words mean so much from Eoin. In Eoin's way, I am like a daughter to him. As my parental figure, he lives in this house for all the requirements of the Terra realm. But it doesn't feel like just a legal relationship. I trust him.

"So, can I ask you something?" He nods. "Can you tell me anything regarding my parents and Paris?"

Eoin's shoulders stiffen at my question. "Maybe this is something you should ask Sabine about. She is, after all, your grandmother and understands the story at a different level. My view is purely a military one."

"So does that mean you're not gonna tell me? I don't think I can ask Sabine. I think she will shut down as soon as I ask her. Besides, Evan doesn't trust her, and although she's changed from who she was in the past or is trying to, I'm not sure—"

I cut myself off. I cannot believe I just said that out loud. Eoin doesn't seem shocked by my comments at all though. Does that mean he doesn't trust her either?

Eoin gathers our plates and starts washing them in the sink. Not looking at me, he begins. "The Wiccan King commanded the Guardians to retrieve Nuala and kill whoever interfered. She was on the run with a bounty on the head of your father; the complete order said he forced Nuala against her will. The assumption was that he had bewitched her. They were located near Paris and a large battle ensued. Souls were lost and your father was wounded—by my hand. It was a family squabble turned into a military operation. I do regret that, Willow." He looks at me finally, his eyes sad at his admission. "However, there is no room for discussion or push back with a King's orders."

He looks at me as he dries off the dishes, his eyes a little softer around the edges. "Your mother was very powerful, although not as powerful as you, and she broke through the spell that prevented transportation. It's a spell we do when we are going after Wiccans and other magical creatures so that there's no easy getaway. By breaking that, many were able to escape. It was the start of what we called the Great Hunt. It became clear that Nuala did have free will and was clearly attached to your father, revealing that the King had other intentions against his headstrong daughter."

After seeing Evan's memory of Mr. Boward and my mother, I certainly understand my mother fleeing. My father would have never bewitched her. I'm sure Harkin and Sabine would have known this as well.

"You have to understand, the Guardians are loyal to the crown. There are laws to enforce, but you do not disobey direct orders from the one who wears the crown."

"Do you think that is right? For me to give orders to the Guardians unchallenged? I don't know anything about the military. I don't want that power."

Eoin shrugs but looks directly in my eyes. "I've never had the option of talking about my opinions in twenty-five years as a Guardian. But I think you need to be very careful after last night's encounter with the phantom. The Emissaries are expanding their hate crimes against Wiccans. It seems that it's not a time to be too radical—but then again, maybe it's the perfect time."

I like this Eoin, not dictating orders as he does with Rhydian, Cross, Tullen, and Quinn, but just chatting like we're friends.

"Do you think the Emissaries are bad?" Eoin raises his eyebrow but doesn't respond. "I honestly want your opinion."

He scratches the incoming growth on his chin. "I believe that here, you would call them protestors. I don't think they are bad, but some of their methods are extreme and lead to dangerous outcomes. Maybe a more fitting description is that they rebel against the status quo of royal rule and Wiccan superiority."

"Eoin, I rebel against the status quo myself. Does that make me part of the Emissaries? For that matter, my mother was next in line, and as I understand, she would have taken the crown. I have the feeling both she and my father held similar beliefs—she could have ended Wiccan superiority. Is that why she was killed?"

Eoin's eyes are dark and soft. "The Great Hunt was a cleansing of those who rose against the crown and Wiccan rule in Edayri. It signaled the formal start of the Emissaries, whose beliefs would have ended the power cycle within Wiccan families. Willow, I think your mother was going to take the crown, but it was clear she and Aiden had a different idea of how Edayri should be governed. It caused a rocky family dynamic. Those in the High Coven have motive for ensuring the crown continues in their favor, complete with a magickal power that is bound to and used by royalty. A hierarchy that's no longer needed?" He whistles low. "There are a lot who wouldn't stand for that. They have too much to lose." Eoin's smile is soft and reassuring. "But then again, a seventeen-year-old came into the Hallowed Hall, disbanded the High Coven in one night, and was crowned by the Goddess, so that's already rocked the foundation of tradition."

"I almost didn't accept the crown. Hell, I think about that day a lot—destiny and all that."

"You assume destiny requires your permission to exist. It doesn't. There is always someone who will battle those who are hungry for power and status," Eoin says.

Am I hungry for power?

Yes.

CHAPTER 15

Late Sunday afternoon, I'm called back to MacKinnon Manor. Sabine is adamant I return for training and a meeting with her because of the phantom situation at Coral's party. I'm leery of the intention since she also requested I bring Duke with me. I have a terrible feeling my return to Chepstow will not be in time for school tomorrow.

Mr. Boward enters the office suites just after I arrive. Duke growls when he enters. The tall man eyes him and Duke settles. "The party that you and Rhydian went to yesterday evening—how was it?"

"It was a good party." I shrug and pet Duke from my chair. I don't want to reveal anything about Lucy and the phantom attack. If I do, he may use that information to keep me in Edayri full-time.

Mr. Boward sits across from me and leans forward, interlacing his fingers. "Rhydian did provide a full report to his commanding officer, and since I'm acting as your Scepter, I have access to all reports."

Shit. Rhydian's commanding officer is Eoin. I sit back in my chair and let the curved high back hug my shoulders.

"I'm thankful that you were with Rhydian. It could have been an unmanageable situation. And considering others were attending who could have been injured, it would have been—"

I cut him off, flustered. "I don't know what details you have access to, but everything has been taken care of and is fine."

"Willow, it is important that we have trust and transparency. I'm just learning that you are close to valkyries and shapeshifters? Who would have thought such powerful beings would be in the Terra realm and make themselves known to you." Mr. Boward's tone is smug.

Is this a challenge of knowledge? Does he want me to share those details? My blood starts to boil as he looks down his nose at me for what happened at the party.

"Is this a test? Interesting. You're not so forthcoming yourself. You were betrothed to my mother, and you fell to a lower coven status once she left you for my father. Why didn't you reveal that to me?" I pause, watching his eyes change from soft edges to a hard determination. "Are we working on trust and transparency?" I stand and walk to the big bay window that overlooks the grounds. The window's reflection shows me that my magick is flowing on my skin, which satisfies me.

Yes—show him who you are.

"That's fair. I was friends with your father, and I loved your mother most of my life. It wasn't a returned affection, but I didn't do anything to upset my friendship with your parents. They were both dear to me. I did marry and have my own children, Willow. I have my own life story."

"Why didn't you say anything to me before?"

"To be frank, I told you we grew up together. Your mother—what was I to say? She married your father, and I married Vanessa. It was a lifetime ago."

Esmund stands next to me and gestures back to the chair. "I suppose we are working on trust and transparency, but I think current events are relevant when your safety is in jeopardy. Based on the report, it was." I say nothing. After a moment, he says, "Are you ready for your lessons today?" He looks every bit the uptight college professor I'd imagined I would have next year in his dark pants, white oxford shirt, and brown jacket.

Will I even get to go to college?

"We have a fun-filled afternoon of royal history and a few papers for you to sign . . ."

I don't listen to him drone on. All I can seem to focus on is what next year might be like and how I will possibly manage. Mr. Boward's mouth is moving, but I'm not registering anything he's saying, it's as if the sound has been sucked out of the room. I will have to be in Edayri full-time next year; I'm expected to be here. Will I ever see my school friends? I will see Emily. Maybe Marco? The change is so hard to wrap my mind around.

He clears his throat before I hear, "Willow? What did I just say?"

Busted.

Mr. Boward is frowning, forehead crinkled as he waits. His eyes are similar to Rhydian's, but not the same—the luster of a hazel storm mixed with blue, green, and gold is flat and dull.

"Um, sorry."

"I thought so. I know the legions of the lunar fields are not exciting stuff, but this is important Wiccan history."

I nod and open my eyes wide to focus. He's right, it's not exciting stuff at all—the takeover and domination of the moon fairies. Or rather, as he puts it, the "organization and peacekeeping mission for the benefit of the once-mischievous fairies who were ill-equipped and unfocused."

"Yes, it is important. I'm sorry, Mr. Boward."

"Please, if you insist I call you Willow, will you please call me Esmund? After all, you are dating my son, and I am your Scepter."

He smiles, but his eyes seem indifferent to me, like it's all an act or performance he's grown accustomed to.

"I'll try."

❧

By the time I leave the office suite, I'm wound tight. A smiling Rhydian approaches me. "Hey." His eyes change from joy to concern when he reaches for my hand.

I pull back; I don't want him to sense my feelings. I try to block him searching me, my magick already flowing, but it doesn't matter because his father opens the door.

"Hello, son." He nods to me and smiles. "Willow." He adjusts the leather satchel over his shoulder and walks down the hall.

I weakly return Rhydian's smile.

"Everything okay?"

Truthfully, I can't wait to hit something—hard. Gah! Mr. Boward—Esmund—is so frustrating. It gives me the creeps to think of him by his first name. How can he be Rhydian's father? Talk about polar opposites—or maybe not? That thought is scrubbed from my mind as soon as it comes.

"I'm running late. I'm meeting Cross for combat training." I try to leave but Rhydian grabs my hand.

"Want me to take you?"

"No, no, that's fine. I know where I'm going." I gently pull my hand from his. "I'll catch you later." I quickly walk down the hall out of sight, then transport into the gym locker room.

Cross wastes no time. We shuffle on the mat. I land punches and kick as directed. I revel in it— there's no thinking required, and I get to hit something.

"High, low, right, left, high knee . . ."

I'm more confident and landing every hit and kick.

Cross counters in offensive moves. I'm prepared and block. His big body directs me toward a wall. I duck and slide under him, and his eyes grow wide and appreciative.

"Oh no, I'm not being directed today." I huff and jump side to side, knocking my gloved hands together.

"Excellent," Cross says with a smirk. He continues to attack, and we go back and forth.

Three rounds later, both Cross and I drip in sweat.

"Yer confidence and abilities are improving in just weeks. It's impressive."

I agree. I don't feel helpless. If I don't have magick, I can fight. I will fight, because, damn it, I'm a fighter.

I help Cross clear the equipment in the room.

"So, what's going on with you and Emily? Any interest there?"

His eyes light up at her name. "Yeah, for sure. She's amazing, not to mention not bad on the eyes."

"Really, you're that superficial?" I laugh and push him.

Holding his hands up, he steps back with a laugh. "Nah, not at all. She's a warrior like me and, well, I love me." He winks.

"Apparently. No overinflated ego here."

"What! No ego, just truth." He flexes his arm and nods in appreciation.

We put the last of the extra mats in the wall locker and he closes the door.

"What about what Marco said yesterday?" I'm surprised to hear Marco's name from Cross. "Do you think someone is conjuring phantom's?"

"I would guess it's possible. Emily isn't happy about it."

"Ya think it's a schoolmate of yours?"

My thoughts go to Coral. She wasn't frozen, but it still seems crazy to think of her. Maybe someone else? Cross can't be too off; just look at Marco and Emily. There is no telling who else might be magickal.

I shrug. "I guess it could be? I don't know. How would I be able to tell?"

"There would be a magical signature, but to follow it would be hard, especially when you're battling the phantom."

"A magickal signature?"

"Yeah. I imagine with yer power, ya could tap into seeing the threads of magick that they're using. The phantom's like a puppet. Trace it back to a source." He shrugs. "If it's conjured, that is. Someone's gotta be commanding it. Rhy and I thought it could be possible."

My heart softens a bit at the mention of Rhydian.

"I hope not to see another one, but if I do, maybe I could look for the signature."

Cross claps me on the back, and we go in different directions toward the locker rooms.

I change and look for Sabine in her office. It's empty. I spy books stacked on the bureau and pick them up. The one that catches my eye and stops me cold is titled *Apparitions and Phantoms*. Sabine walks in with her assistant.

"Training is done for the day?" she asks, walking to her desk and sitting in a high-back chair.

"Yes, I suppose so, unless you have something else on my schedule."

She doesn't catch my sarcasm, or if she does, she ignores it.

"No, actually. I just want to ensure you and Esmund met today."

"Okay." I roll my eyes.

She finally looks at me and dismisses her assistant.

"What happened?"

"He wants more trust and transparency." I study her face, but it's indifferent.

"Well, it's suitable for his role."

"So I'm told." I sit in front of her. "How did he become Scepter?"

"I appointed him. I can't be everywhere, and I need someone who knows the crown's formality and will help you."

"That would be Eoin, not Mr. Boward."

Sabine huffs at me. "Eoin is the commander of the Guardians." She waves her hand in the air dismissively. "He has a huge responsibility outside of acting as your Terra realm parental Guardian."

"You're right. In my world, I would have a family member as a parental Guardian. Plus, I'm dating Rhydian, and this is just weird!"

For once, Sabine doesn't have an immediate response. A good thirty seconds go by before she asks, slyly, "So, you're dating?"

I nod and can't help mirroring the small grin on her face.

"Stop," I laugh. "Yes, we are dating, and I like

Rhydian. A lot." Her grin spreads and so does mine. "Okay. Stop it."

She shakes her head and brings us out of our grinning showdown. "Esmund has arranged a big meeting tomorrow with the former high council and noble coven families without our invitation. I suspect they will try to reinstate the high council. There is a movement to move the crown out of the family. It's a rumor, but I believe that Esmund is seeding it. He can be quite persuasive."

"You don't trust him and you want to keep him close?" As I say it, relief floods me. Talk about keeping enemies close. Is he a real enemy?

"I trust him to protect himself, but you're not off-base."

"I don't want to be directed by him anymore. I can't be some royal dictator to everyone in this realm. I'm not Harkin, and it's not right. This tears apart everything. If this place is to survive in harmony with everyone, there has to be a change."

I'm prepared for a verbal battle with her, but she smiles gently at me and says, "Yes, I know."

"Then why are you letting Mr. Boward in so close?"

"Willow, not all storms come to disrupt your life. Some come to clear your path. Have some patience, but with open eyes. Esmund is someone to keep an eye on."

I sure hope the storm that's coming isn't a category six hurricane, because there may be nothing left.

PART III

By knot of six, this spell I fix
By knot of seven, events I'll leaven

CHAPTER 16

On Monday, Sabine and I leave MacKinnon Manor together for the first time and transport to the Hallowed Hall. The Hallowed Hall is the center point of Edayri, like a capital building. The white marble, columns, and Goddess fountain are a shining symbol of Wiccan rule. The Guardian headquarters are attached to the west.

We have a plan and are not going to be blindsided. Sabine agrees the royal rule of solidarity needs to change; she is entirely supportive. I want to heed Evan's warnings, but I can't. Sabine says the magical ties that bind us to Edayri should be honored; otherwise, someone will chance a claim.

The only part I'm not overly confident about is staying ahead of Mr. Boward and the former High Coven members. This quorum is for hearing proposals for the reworking of the royal governances. Still, Sabine feels the noble covens will make a move for the high council because of the draw of magickal position and influence.

Political games.

"Good afternoon." Eoin is waiting when we arrive. We have transported to a back entrance near the Guardian training grounds, so our arrival isn't noticed by the quorum. "Are you ready?"

"Yes." My voice sounds more confident than I feel. Eoin smiles and nods, utterly aware of our plan.

"Let's go through the back passages so that we can be announced ahead of the quorum opening," Sabine directs.

"It will be more inconspicuous if I'm not leading you. I have ordered Quinn and Tullen to meet us halfway."

Sabine and I follow Eoin, making quick work of the twisting tunnels beneath the Hallowed Hall. When we reach Quinn and Tullen, Eoin touches my shoulder and looks directly into my eyes. "Good luck. Remember who you are. Don't let them get the sense they can control you." Nodding to everyone else, he walks back in the direction we came from.

No one says anything as we continue down the passageway. Tullen is in front of us, Quinn behind. We start on an upward walk that drives us closer to the audience room where the meeting is being held. Instead of coming into the hallway from the front doors, we enter from behind the throne and raised stage.

Mr. Boward turns to watch us enter just as he is calling the opening of the quorum. His lips purse close. The doors shut, and Eoin follows procedure and enters from the side. Mr. Boward's eyes follow Eoin, who comes to stand next to Sabine.

Instead of calling the quorum, he takes a moment to come to the throne. "I see we still need to work on transparency."

"Yes, I believe we do," I reply.

"Sabine? Should I call an end to the quorum? The one, I might add, that you once assembled as a former high council member?" Mr. Boward's smirk hovers on manipulation. Still, I stay steady, staring ahead at the large audience of noble coven attendees in front of us.

"Oh Esmund, I think you can continue, but as you know, the high council was abolished by Willow when she accepted the crown. The Guardians are here just in case there is any trouble. This quorum of noble coven members is important to the crown. It is such a good thing we learned of it just in time to attend."

He looks like a fish for a second, as if he'd been about to reply with a witty retort but thought better of it. Mr. Boward turns on his heel and speaks into a microphone at the end of the raised floor.

"As above and below, I call this official quorum into order as Scepter to the crown." There is the sound of a bell in the back of the room. Everyone in attendance sits, robes of various colors fluttering. The looks on the faces nearest to me are almost enter-taining—the wide eyes, parted lips, and nervous wringing of hands.

Mr. Boward stands still for a moment before

Sabine interrupts the silence. "Shall we proceed, Scepter?"

"Yes, thank you." He clears his throat. "The call to quorum is to hear the reinstatement of the high council. Please bring forth your declarations for the crown."

A previous High Coven member, Renata, stands. I remember her by her distinct white hair, striking in its spiky fashion.

Her eyes move from me to Sabine. "The high council would request a vote of abdication of Willow Warrington from the throne so that Sabine may continue in the royal rule."

The gasps throughout the room are audible. My focus is on Renata. She steps back, and it's clear her bravery is only on the surface of her words.

I wonder if Sabine anticipated this. Would she stay on the path we agreed or take a new direction to become Queen? Pansy, another previous High Coven member, vocalizes her agreement in a high pitched, nervous voice. When I look at her, she shrinks in her seat. I can't help the smile that creeps into the corners of my mouth.

They should be scared of me.

There is a rumbling of voices and Mr. Boward says, "We have a motion which makes to reinstitute our esteemed high council. Based on recent events—"

Eoin interrupts. "As Scepter, your role is not directive but only informative to the crown. As she is present, the quorum will now be informed." The satisfaction in Eoin's eyes is rewarding to watch Mr. Boward retreat from.

"Of course, of course."

"It seems I have crashed the party today," I say. I stand up, and, with my magick flowing to show my crown clearly, I steady my nerves. I push my shoulders back so that I stand tall. "The proposal to vote for the reinstatement of the high council is no longer applicable. This council was abolished with my acceptance of the crown. The fact that it has continued to be pressed in quorums behind my back could be considered treason."

Gasps echo throughout the audience room. Guardians have been placed at the entrances and the room is under a spell to prevent transportation. The faces are priceless, mostly of fear—a few look on more curiously. The noise level rises to a dull roar.

Mr. Boward speaks up. "If it pleases the crown, may we have a private word? This was a peaceful meeting of declaration and discussion."

I ignore him, and Sabine stares ahead without acknowledgment.

"Do I have your attention?" I wait until the noise subsides. "I am instituting an equalized representation for a self-governing society. The royal rule will remain in the background, used only for tie breaks and oversight as majority rules. The Guardians will serve society, and a small contingency will continue to serve the Royal family—the Royal Guardians, as already named."

I have practiced this, and I was focused and

unrushed. I am more empowered than I ever have been.

You are power.

"A bold move, and one that would bring old traditions and new ones together. It is time to come out of the past and grow to the future," Sabine says.

The eyes that look back at me are wide. Mr. Boward is lifting his chin and staying quiet as if he is in on this arrangement. Everyone is stunned into silence.

"Who among you would be willing to support the crown in building this new governing body? Understand that others within Edayri will be in this governing body—fairies, demons, and the like. This will be a body not overrun by one group, but a balanced mix of all."

"I would." The voice comes from the back. I recognize Aren, another former high council member. She was the one I met who seemed misplaced in the high council of older women and who looked so bored the last time I saw her. She walks forward, shoving away from an older female who reaches for her. "This has been a long time coming," Aren says as she approaches us.

"Thank you, Aren." A rumble begins to spread throughout the room as others are pulled from their stunned silence.

"As Scepter, I will support you in whatever way you see fit," Mr. Boward says, then bows to me.

Sabine puts her hand on his shoulder and says quietly, "We should talk privately."

The quorum ends peacefully without more attempts to abdicate me or establish some grand overthrowing of power. Instead, we leave with two Wiccan representatives, one a former High Coven member and one a younger noble coven member. Next, Ax will reach out to the demons and others to find representatives for the new governing body of Edayri.

CHAPTER 17

I'm back at Trinity Cross High School on Tuesday. Mrs. Gunther, the civics teacher, is droning on about the Depression era in the United States, noting a direct correlation between the economy and the culture of warfare, as well as its effect on future days. Typically, I would be listening to Mrs. Gunther because she always has interesting parallels in class, and you don't want to be caught off guard when she calls on you. But the way Coral keeps side-eyeing me from her desk has my attention elsewhere. Usually, she's looking over at Rhydian or one of her friends, but Rhydian isn't in school today. Mr. Boward requested him for some important task today that Eoin begrudgingly allowed. Why do I have her full attention?

"Willow, if the crash of the 1940s were to happen today, what would be the first to fall in our current economy?"

Darn it. I knew she would target me. "I would

anticipate the downfall of the free market. I would also expect that societal prejudices might be reintroduced." Edayri would be the same.

"Ah, so you are listening." She pauses, looking out the window. "Interesting thought that prejudices would be reintroduced to society. The scale of those prejudices would be based on what? Coral?"

"Fear. Most prejudice is based on fear, but then, of course, the power of influence and money ensures it."

I'm unsurprised by Coral's response, but she isn't wrong. Here, despite the regulation school uniforms, family wealth and names dictate your status in the social hierarchy. I rebel against the school uniforms with my purple Converse, but Coral's rebellion is made up of high-end backpacks, expensive jewelry, and expensive makeup. There's an expectation to flaunt your wealth, which is just ridiculous. Still, Coral and her cronies live and die by the social popularity of success of the school.

Coral is staring at me again, her eyes a bit wider. She seems to be tilting her head, trying to communicate with me, but I don't understand. I mouth the word "what?"

She circles her face with her finger. Her eyes look worried and not condescending. Something is on my face?

Before I can do anything, I hear the hum. As soon as I'm alerted to it, I notice my magick growing. The designs on my hands glow faintly under the skin. Coral can see it, but she doesn't seem to be disturbed by it. I realize that she is watching my forehead, where my crown would be starting to show.

I need to leave.

Not wanting to call attention to myself, I pull my hair from its ponytail and pull the strands forward. Coral rolls her eyes. I can't believe she's halfway trying to help me.

No one else notices me; everyone is focused on Mrs. Gunther. Maybe I can put a spell on the room so that no one will see?

Before I can think much further, the entire school shakes. It feels like an earthquake, like nothing I've ever felt living in Massachusetts. The hair on my neck is rising at the sense of something magickal.

Mrs. Gunther shouts, "Everyone stay calm. We need to move out of this room and down the hall in an orderly fashion—"

The window along the outside wall cracks and a girl next to it yelps. Everyone scrambles from their seats. The fire alarms go off at a second shake of the room. It's hard to stay upright; a few students fall to their knees. Mrs. Gunther raises her voice above the piercing alarm. "Leave everything. Meet me in parking lot B, now!" She grabs a clipboard by the classroom door just as the windows break with a great burst of air.

I instinctively throw my hands out to stop the momentum of the glass. The wind is a funnel of pressure that pushes Mrs. Gunther out of the room with half the class and slams the door, leaving myself, Coral, and a few of my classmates inside. I drop my hands, and the remaining glass falls. Steve tries the door and yells that is locked, then begins beating on it with another student.

The lights flicker off. A dark, gauze-like material hovers like fog around a corpse form. The phantom enters the class through the window and shrieks, "Thhee Wicccannn Queeeen."

Another phantom sweeps in with a long, high-pitched shriek that drowns the screams of my fellow classmates.

One phantom rushes at the door and grabs Steve, who is blocking it.

My chest is pounding in my ears. My hands are shaking.

Show them.

Coral reaches for my arm. "Be careful," she stammers, kneeling behind an overturned desk.

I gather my magick and move between the overturned desks toward the front of the classroom. I push my hands toward the floor with a scream; everything touching the floor except my classmates is thrown into the air in a quick snap, then falls again.

I grab the air that I've gathered and throw it out the window along with the phantoms. The classroom shakes again. Everyone seems to be unconscious on the floor except Coral, who is barely holding on.

"Who are you?" Coral asks weakly.

I consider her. Why is she being helpful? I can't take the risk. I can remove this memory like I did with Daniel. I begin to move my magick, designs flowing on my arms. Coral pushes herself up and yells,

"No! You tell me how it happened at my party. I have proof on my phone."

"Coral, we don't have time for this—"

Someone is yelling in the hallway. I flip my hand, and the door is thrown off the hinges, slamming into the whiteboard behind where Mrs. Gunter's desk used to be. Cross runs in dressed as a fireman and motions for us to move. I help Coral up and she leans into me. Cross easily hefts Steve over his shoulder as the others wake.

We follow Cross. The hallways are full of papers, books, glass, and rubble. Dust is everywhere, like an eerie fog. Doors are flung open, the floor is uneven and broken, and the lights flicker on and off.

I've pulled back my magick so that I'm no longer lit up like a Christmas tree, but I have to concentrate. Most of my classmates are well ahead of us. To my relief, most of the school is already outside when we reach the parking lot.

I help Coral to a curb. "Tell me and I'll forget what I saw, but never use your witchy powers on me," Coral says, smirking.

Cross laughs, then bends his towering, muscled frame over her and whispers, "Willow can do whatever she feels like, so best be careful when tryin' to blackmail her. Maybe ya should just say 'thank ya.'"

Coral's face is pale, and her mouth opens, clearly in disbelief that Cross knows my name.

"Coral, don't—ugh—Cross?" I can't believe he just said that.

Coral's eyes are wide, but the audible gulp makes Cross laugh louder. "Thank you," she says.

He shrugs and touches his earpiece. "Copy that." He turns to me. "You stay here. I've got to go back to the east wing." He runs off. The lights of fire trucks, police cars, and ambulances are all around us, along with television crews.

"Listen, Coral, I do need you to keep quiet about me." I plead with my eyes.

"Willow—I will. Thank you again."

"I bet that tasted awful to say to me." I smile weakly.

"Yep." She nods as Mrs. Gunter yells our names, and we respond together. "Here."

CHAPTER 18

My mind is filled with the echo of the last several hours. Sitting alone in the receiving room at MacKinnon Manor, I see the dirt and dust, smell the smoke, hear the fire alarm and the screams, watch the terror on my classmates' faces. I keep replaying the phantoms busting through the glass. They were there for me, not Lucy. But Lucy was at school. Is she okay? What about Daniel, Marco, and Emily? I didn't find them in the school parking lot. Everyone is a blur of faces in my memory—classmates, teachers, parents, first responders—until the moment Eoin signed me out and I transported here.

I jump when Rhydian and Eoin enter.

Rhydian reaches me in two giant steps. "Oh Goddess, Willow."

He's wet and covered in dirt; he must have come from the school. He pulls me to his body in a hug, and I cling to him. "The school's foundation on the east side has crumbled completely. Several students were injured. Your friends are okay—Lucy, Marco, and Daniel."

I only realize I'm shaking when I pull away, then collapse back into him. I've almost forgotten Eoin is in the room when he speaks.

"Willow."

My eyes follow his voice to find him not far from where Rhydian and I stand.

"I'm sorry, but the student from your class, Steve, is in the hospital. He's not conscious; it's not clear if he will wake up."

Steve. An image flashes in my mind of Cross carrying him over his shoulder out of the school.

"How? Why did this happen?" Tears are streaming down my face. I wipe them away as quickly as they fall. Stepping away from the comfort of Rhydian, I hug myself. "I should have acted faster. I tried to protect my identity, but my magick was warning me, and I didn't pick up on it. It's my—"

"It's the phantoms' fault," Eoin interrupts. "Along with whoever is controlling them."

I can't go back to Chepstow. I would be putting everyone at risk. At least here in Edayri, there are Guardians, and I can use my magick freely. I drop onto the french sateen bench, my mind spiraling.

"Willow, I have several people looking into this. For now, you will only be in Chepstow if multiple backups are always present. It was a mistake not to have Rhydian on campus today. Ax, Cross, Tullen, and Quinn will work backup rotations with other Guardians for support." Eoin continues to update me on the status of the school. It's been heavily damaged by fire and smoke. The blame is being placed on a fault line and an overrun electrical power grid—the perfect storm for Trinity Cross High. The story has already been casting at local and national levels.

I only catch bits and pieces of his words. My thoughts go back to the classroom. My magick tried to warn me before it all went to hell. What else am I not paying attention to that I should be noticing?

"How about you come to my home for dinner? Get out of your head and here?" Rhydian asks.

Still hugging myself, I take a deep breath. "Yes, okay. Let me change and talk with Sabine."

I'm dreading talking with Sabine. She was right; I need to be here. I put everyone in danger with my selfish need to keep my old life.

Eoin speaks up. "Sabine is meeting with Thaxam about representation in the newly established government. By the way, they've adopted the name 'Legion Council.' She won't be back till late. I'll advise her further before you leave with Rhydian."

Rhydian touches his earpiece. "Come through again. Okay, I'll grab it from you in ten. Yeah, Cross got it."

"What?" My heart is pounding. Please don't let it be—

"Cross has your cell. I'll pick it up for you. That way you can connect with your friends tonight too. Emily is staying with Lucy." Rhydian grins. "Oh, by the way, school is closed for the rest of the week."

My mind is stuck on the comment about my

phone. The ability to contact my friends is a blessing. Tears well in my eyes again. "Thank Cross for my phone and the update."

Later, in the shower, I crumble on the tiled floor and hug my knees. The water slowly takes the dirt and mud to the drain. Death is following me. I can only hope Steve isn't another causality. I was too slow, just like with Mrs. Scott and my father. This is my new norm, and it is crippling. I shake and sob beneath the shield of cold water, letting it all wash down the drain.

Rhydian and I transport to his home in the Guardian housing near the Hallowed Hall. The housing reminds me of row housing in the suburbs. Inside, it is warm and cozy without an ounce of pretension. Overstuffed couches and chairs in dark grays and neutral colors are complemented by splashes of vibrant color in the pillows and abstract art on the walls. I'm not sure how I envisioned Rhydian's space, but this seems to match him.

Mr. Boward welcomes us at the doorway where I imagine his idea of casual clothes—dark slacks, a sweater vest, and a collared shirt. I hear a female voice call out, and I realize that Rhydian's sister is here too.

"Abigail?"

Before Rhydian can answer me, the voice calls, "Yes, and I've been looking forward to meeting you too."

When she comes into view, I recognize her immediately. She was at the campsite where the Emissaries were. She was talking to and taking care of Evan in the memory he showed me! I'm stunned to the spot as she extends her hand to me.

"I'm pleased to meet you. I'm Abigail, but I hope you'll call me Abby."

She doesn't seem much older than Rhydian. Shaking her soft hand, I try to act as normal as possible. Do Mr. Boward and Rhydian know she is in the Emissaries? Would it matter now that things are changing for Edayri rule? Evan trusts her.

"Nice to meet you, Abby. Hello Mr.—ah, Esmund."

We all sit down in an alcove near the kitchen for dinner. Rhydian and Abigail set out a roasted chicken with vegetables and bread. Rhydian cuts the meat and places some on my plate.

"Abigail here works in the Hallowed Hall as a coordinator in the finance department."

"Actually, dad, I'm doing something a bit new now. The department is evolving, and I volunteered to be part of the coordination group to integrate the new council."

The look on Mr. Boward's face is one of shock and a trace of disappointment. Abby continues to eat and shrugs her shoulders, dismissively at her father.

"I thought you had advancement opportunities already within your department? Why make this move? It is not what I would call stable. It adds no real value. Well, what I mean is—"

"I think you may have just insulted the crown for which you work," Abby teases, looking at me.

Rhydian chuckles and squeezes my hand under the table. "Father, times are changing. I commend Abby. It's good to see everyone coming together, embracing change."

"Look! Even the exalted son, with all his advancements in traditional rank, agrees." Abby smirks and continues to eat.

I want to stay invisible during this conversation, but Mr. Boward's eyes are on me.

"No, you're right, absolutely right," he says. "This is a wonderful opportunity for the family."

Abby smiles again in a mocking way. "Yes, a wonderful opportunity for me."

"Isn't that what I said?" Mr. Boward stands and clears his plate. He asks Rhydian to help with the table.

The tension is palpable. Rhydian's right—Abby knows how to push her father's buttons. She's an adult and clearly living her own life; I envy her that independence. Although I want to continue to eat the food on my plate, I push it off to the side.

"Sorry about that. The old man is full of old traditions, and it will take a little bit of time for him to come around. Stubborn as a mule, that one."

I drop my voice. "Does he know that you're part of the Emissaries? Or, for that matter, does Rhydian?"

Abigail leans forward and, in a hushed voice, says, "This is still illegal, so no, they do not. If you can keep that between us, that would be great. I would hate to be taken in by both of them tonight. It would certainly put a damper on the evening."

Illegal? How is it illegal? I don't have time to ask because Mr. Boward and Rhydian return with dessert.

"Do you like cheesecake?" Rhydian asks, setting a large piece in front of me with syrupy purple fruit drizzled on top.

"Oh, Abigail is famous for it." Mr. Boward says.

I take a bite, and the cheesecake melts in my mouth. "Oh Goddess. This is incredible!" I look at Abigail in wonder. "How do you get it to be so fluffy and dense all at the same time?"

They all laugh at me, and the tension in the room seems to lift. We make jokes and lighthearted comments throughout the rest of dessert, Rhydian and I teasing each other more than the others.

"I'm so happy at how well you both get along. Aiden would've loved to have seen this."

"Father," Rhydian says in a warning tone. Abby absentmindedly stirs her coffee.

"I'm sure he would've loved to have had dinner here tonight with his old friend. I do miss him a great deal." For a moment, he looks regretful and sincere.

Mr. Boward and Rhydian get up to clear the dessert dishes. I start to follow them with my own when Abby stops me.

"Be careful of my father. His motives are never for the greater good; they're always for the betterment of himself. I love my father, but I'm certain of this, and you should second-guess everything he does and says."

I'm stunned. In thirty seconds, Abby is telling me

to be wary of her father. I already am, of course, but is this a trick? I don't think so. I could reveal her as part of the Emissaries right now to her father and brother. She's got nothing to gain by warning me.

Rhydian appears from around the corner. "What's taking you guys so long?" He grabs the two plates from our hands and disappears back into the kitchen.

"Abby—"

"Forgive me. I wasn't sure when I'd have the opportunity, and the night's almost over. Just one last thing—Evan sends his good wishes. And I'm delighted you're in Rhydian's life." She smiles and encompasses me in a hug that I am entirely unprepared for.

When he joins us again, Rhydian is all smiles and completely relaxed. I say farewell to Mr. Boward and Abby as they settle down in the sitting area near the fireplace.

Outside, Rhydian takes my hands in his. "So, back to MacKinnon Manor?"

My magick flows on my skin. I meet his eyes with mine. The way he looks at me and all he does provides a feeling of protection and respect that I want to soak up and never let go of. I hesitate to go back to MacKinnon Manor and revisit the day's events, but there is no escaping them.

"Yes, I guess so."

We transport to the front steps of the manor. The gas lamps illuminate the entryway.

"Thanks for coming to dinner tonight at my home. You're welcome anytime." His eyes move from my eyes to my lips.

"You have a lovely home. Thank—"

Rhydian's lips are on mine, cutting off my words. His kiss is claiming and my return just as urgent. I can drown in his affection. His kiss creates a sensation that reaches all the way to my toes. My mind is quiet, full only of wonder.

"Willow—"

Hearing my name, feeling the absence of his lips on mine, my brain fills with all the doubts that were drowned just moments before.

"Willow, I need to go back home, but damn. I would stay here on your steps all night with you if I could."

Looking in his eyes, I tamper down my emotions. "Okay. I should probably go inside then."

"Yeah." His hands still steady on my waist, and I don't move. After a beat, his hands fall, and I back toward the door.

"Thank you, Rhydian, for dinner." I smile, and he waves awkwardly. I laugh.

"Anytime," he smiles, then transports away.

CHAPTER 19

I t's been over two weeks since the incident at the
school. This is my first time out of Edayri. Quinn
looks out of place following Emily and me to various
dress stores in the mall, an outing prompted by Emily.
Despite the school's initial cancelation of prom,
Coral's family put up the money for a swanky hotel
and additional security. So, prom is happening, and
dress shopping is on. For me, though, it's more about
hanging with Emily the way we did before all the
magickal craziness of our lives—well, my life. I wish
Lucy had joined us, but she is continuing to keep a
distance from Emily.

"I'm starting to feel bad for him," Emily says,
interrupting my thoughts. "He's gotta be extremely
bored."

Quinn pokes his head between Emily and me. "If I
may, I suggest we go to another location. These
dresses are not what I would call fashionable or suited
for you, lovely ladies." I look at him, eyes wide.

"There are three shops in Town Center that you should consider. You will find a unique and lovely dress at any one of them."

"Okay. And how exactly do you know this?" Emily asks with her hand on her hip.

"I've had to escort noble covens before. Let's just say this isn't my first dress shopping assignment, and Town Center is definitely better than here."

I can't help but chuckle at Quinn's dress shopping expertise. We all agreed to go.

Quinn drives us in a large SUV like political dignitaries who require high-security vehicles. Since it means I'm allowed back in the Terra realm, I won't complain.

"If you had to choose between the Terra realm or Edayri, which would you choose?" Emily asks Quinn.

He ponders her question for a moment. "They each offer something different. Because I grew up in Edayri, you think I'd want to stay. But it seems like there are so many more freedoms here in the Terra realm. So, if I had to choose one and never see the other . . . It would break my heart, but I would probably choose here."

I'm surprised at Quinn's response. "What types of freedoms are you speaking about?"

He shrugs, keeping his eyes on the road. "Where do I begin? So many political, sexual, religious, and creative freedoms. Because you guys have always had them here, you take them for granted. I understand this isn't the way in all regions of the Terra realm, but still. To be told who you are and how to live and what to believe . . . It makes my skin crawl."

"So, who is he? Or am I reading too much into what you're saying?" Emily asks, smiling.

This seems too invasive of her, but at the same time, I am curious. I would like to know Quinn on a deeper level.

"He's someone of an important position and, although not new, it isn't something I can flaunt openly." Quinn's voice is soft, but he sounds hurt.

"Wow. That sounds heartbreaking, Quinn," I say.

"It is, and it isn't. It depends on how much I overthink it. But if I accept the moments that I have, it's wonderful."

Am I doing the same thing? Am I overthinking myself and Rhydian with the blood vow? Emily certainly thinks so. Maybe I should appreciate our moments for what they are. They are wonderful too.

I settle into thoughts about Rhydian. Quinn isn't talking much either. I assume he's thinking about the guy we were just asking about.

After a while, Quinn takes an exit that I'm unfamiliar with. Several turns later, we arrive in the parking lot for Town Center, an outdoor shopping center with unique boutiques and high-dollar shopping.

The first boutique where Quinn introduces us to the shopkeeper, who, according to him, is the best, has amazing dresses. I'm in a dressing room with two dresses that Quinn helped me pick out. The first one is blue with an empire waist and a lovely, flowing skirt.

The second is a light peach with a sweetheart neck-line and bolts that drape around the dress. Both are stunning. I don't have the green light to even attend prom, but I hope I can go if just for an hour.

When I walk out in the first dress, Quinn smiles. I must admit when I see my reflection in the mirror that he has excellent taste.

"You look stunning. I can't wait to see the sunset dress on you though. I think it will be super flattering with your coloring."

When I slip into the peach-colored dress, I feel myself falling in love with it.

"Get out here! I want to see the dress. I found mine." Emily sings.

"Okay, okay." I fasten the hook on the side and turn, watching the skirt twist with the folds. I can't help but spin again, grinning, mesmerized at the mirror's sight. Yep, this is the one.

When I exit the dressing room, I find Quinn smiling and laughing with Emily. Emily is in a short, black, lacy dress with red ribbon accents. I come up between them, and we all smile.

"So, Quinn saves the day, and we are all ready for our last prom," I say.

"Wow, our last prom. I can't believe the school year is almost over. Wills, do you think you'll be going to college like Lucy?"

I shrug. I am barely managing high school atten-dance and look at what just happened on our closed campus. How could I possibly achieve this on a larger scale—attending college while setting up a new governing body and reviewing laws in Edayri? I want to be selfish, but how many lives would I disrupt for a college experience I wouldn't be able to use in Edayri anyway?

"I think I will defer and decide later."

"Nothing wrong with that, Wills. I'm so done with school. I'd love to check out California if Lucy's okay with me going. I think she's starting to come around anyhow."

I'm happy for them, glad Lucy and Emily are mending their relationship, but deep down, I mourn the loss of both of them already. I try to shake this thought out of my head, but it lingers as we change out of our dresses and go to pay.

❧

Quinn and I return to the MacKinnon Manor and are met by Esmund and Sabine. I'm holding my dress in a garment bag from the store, and Sabine smiles weakly when she sees it.

"How was dress shopping?"

"It is beautiful. I can't wait to wear it, whether at prom or not." I'm hoping she'll come around and let me find a way to go, but I don't want to push my luck.

Mr. Boward grins. "How about you go? I spoke with Eoin, and he's drafting plans to work out security. You could attend for an hour or so."

I can't help smiling even if Sabine is tight-lipped. "Willow, I'm not going to allow this if Eoin cannot execute a solid protection plan for this dance."

I have a real shot getting to go to my senior prom! I keep myself from screaming with excitement. I don't care that it's only for a short time; this is more than I anticipated. Even better, I would get another chance to dance with Rhydian.

"Rhydian is looking forward to taking you to this formal event. Wasn't it originally canceled because of the death at your school?" Mr. Boward asks.

And there it is. That's more like the Mr. Boward, I know. "No one died. Fortunately, Steve Carlin is doing well and is out of the hospital. One of the student's parents contributed a hefty amount to have a prom for the seniors. The money that would have funded the prom is going toward the reconstruction of the campus."

Sabine's eyebrows raise, and she touches a finger to her chin. Mr. Boward says, "Interesting. So, you do plan to go despite the danger that could follow. You'd risk your fellow students and friends to do this?"

Sabine steps in quickly before I can respond. She deters him in a masterful, political way with a conversation about how the replacement of existing governmental structures will work. I lay my dress over a couch and sit next to Sabine.

"I understood this was well underway. What's come up?"

"Because you are split in your availability, we are having discussions about providing executive royal powers to both Esmund and myself to help you govern swiftly while you're at school. We have people in holding cells awaiting judgment for various types of hate crimes."

I hear precisely what Sabine is telling me, but I'm having a hard time believing it. Executive royal powers? Why are these needed? I was putting in place a new structure that would govern over everything. Why do they need this royal piece?

"What types of crimes? Are they considered capital offenses?" I ask.

Sabine says that most are property crimes and other minor offenses.

Mr. Boward scoffs. "Small crimes lead to larger ones, and your rule over these situations will be on symbolic display for all of Edayri. That prom really shouldn't get in the way of anyone's future. If you allow Sabine and me to help you, you can maintain your education in Chepstow and Edayri. While you're away as Scepter, I can manage these small little facets." He waves his hand as if this is a small issue.

I'm being scolded like a child, and his passive-aggressive comments irritate me. Still, he knows he needs my approval for the power he is seeking. After meeting Abigail, I have no question that his request has nothing to do with helping me. Sabine, on the other hand, would help me under the circumstances. It could serve to keep her closer to Mr. Boward if he is doing something suspicious.

"Sabine, can we review after dinner this evening?" I ask, directing away from Mr. Boward's request. The ease with which he puts his fists into his pockets suggests he's irritated. The smirk on my face is one I can't hide.

"Really, Esmund, it will be fine. I can meet you after, and we can do the various processes required for these individuals with Commander Eoin and the Guardians," Sabine says.

A sly smile creeps across his face, giving me the chills. "Willow, it is helpful to use me in all capacities as Scepter, but something is off between us. I hope it has nothing to do with my son?"

"Why would you suggest that? It could have everything to do with the High Coven coup."

Sabine's eyes grow large, and her pursed lips give warning. Mr. Boward seems unaffected by my statement.

He moves to sit across from me and leans in. "I know you've gotten close to each other, and Rhydian is very fond of you. I don't want that to come in the way of our roles and the change of structure that you are trying to implement. He worries that you worry about the blood vow and the future betrothal."

"Esmund," Sabine huffs in warning.

Betrothal? Good grief, I'm seventeen! I can't even fathom the idea of marriage. He's trying to bait me. Abigail was right—he would hurt his own family for power and position. How does Rhydian not see this? Or maybe he's like Abigail and just accepts it?

"No, my relationship with Rhydian doesn't change anything. You and I are still working on transparency, I think. The important part is that Sabine understands the complete structure as well as Aren,

Thaxam, and others starting to form the legion council. I understand that Abigail is doing a wonderful job in her new position." It's a little stab of my own because he has no part in any of these discussions and has very little knowledge in this area.

His raised eyebrow slowly drifts down. It feels like a chess match between us. I don't trust him.

CHAPTER 20

Sitting at the white vanity in my room in Chepstow, I brush my long wet hair. I contemplate prom. The royal Guardians are going with me just to make sure everything happens safely. Eoin has had Guardians busy ahead of prom too, placing enchantments that will shield me in the hotel. Is Sabine right? Am I bringing danger by going? Is it selfish for me to go? I accepted the crown so it would no longer be up for a challenge, but it hasn't done anything to keep others—or even me—safe. Staring at my face, I see the eyes of someone who is naive, still a teenager. I have no life experience beyond a privileged, catered life. That isn't going to change as Queen, but I can't live in a cave. Emily thinks the phantoms are controlled by a powerful Wiccan, which would have to be someone from a noble coven. I wonder if the goal was to come after me, Emily, or to trigger Lucy's valkyrie side. Emily is happy with that outcome, but I'm not sure Lucy is so delighted about it.

"Would you like a virtual chocolate shake? I recall how you love chocolate mint; they might have that." Evan interrupts my thoughts, and my stare fest with my mirror. Instead, I'm at a white, silver-trimmed counter staring at the milkshake machines lined up against the white-and-red tiled wall. The red stool swivels, and I face my uncle in a paper hat, red-and-white striped shirt, and white pants. His name tag reads, Fun-cle. I'm underdressed in my terry cloth bathrobe.

"I'm actually getting ready to go to my senior prom. And I really want to go, but . . ."

"You wonder if danger will follow you and if it's selfish to go?" I nod. "It is." He says this without any amble of sensitivity, merely as a matter of fact. He's right, and so is Sabine. Having them on the same side is not something I even want to think about.

He turns on his red and silver stool. "Willow, you need to understand who you are. It will always bring a sense of danger. You are a Queen. You are powerful, magickal, and not many would challenge you. But here's the thing; do you live atop your throne and do nothing? Or do you live your life?"

Without thought, I say, "I want to live my life, but not at the detriment of harming others around me just because we are in the same location."

Evan smiles, and it reaches his eyes. "I remember Nuala saying something similar before she ran. Don't run. Live, flourish, change."

"I'm not running." I haven't run from any of this! I've dived in the best way I can.

"I've been running, and it's like I'm having an asthma attack, and I don't even have asthma."

I giggle at his comment. Until recently, I never felt that strong or capable, but now, thanks to Cross's training, I do. It isn't that fear has left me, but now I have fighting skills and control. It strikes me that Evan running from something sounds absurd. He's a leader in the Emissaries; what could he possibly be running from?

"What have you been running from?"

Evan holds his chin and closes his eyes. I watch him and wait. When an entire minute has passed, he finally speaks. "The Horned God. Do you know who he is?" I nod and sip my shake. "You may be aware that the Horned God has returned. This was right before the Goddess crowned you, not long after I was crowned by the Horned God. We—you and I, my niece—are intertwined on the path that the Goddess and the Horned God could not travel." He stops and slurps some of his vanilla shake.

"What are we going to do that they couldn't?"

"Come together in forgiveness."

I touch his arm, and my hand goes right through it. We are not in this place, only in the confines of our minds.

"I'm ghosting out, Will." He's laughing like a child. I smile at him weakly as we both fade, and I'm staring at my reflection in the mirror again.

"Thanks, Evan, for the time and advice," I say in my mind.

"Anytime, jellybean. Live and run toward it; don't look back," Evan replies. Before our mind connection fades, I hear other voices talking to him.

Knock knock.

"Come in."

Emily enters holding dress bags, tote bags, and caddies. "So, like, I thought we could get ready together since Cross, and I are your secret security tonight." Her face beams with excitement as she hangs her dress on my door with mine.

"So, Cross? Not Marco?"

She makes like she is swooning. "That man—those eyes and those muscles! A girls got to have some options, so don't you be all judgy."

"Never," I laugh. "I'm happy you came over because me and makeup have a bare-bones relationship," I say, eyeing the makeup caddy that she sets down on my vanity.

"Exactly! Not tonight though. We are glamming it up. Dry that hair, and let's move. We only have a little over an hour."

Emily does her makeup first as I twist my hair in an updo and curl the ends on top of my head with my flat iron.

"So tell me, how's it going with Rhydian? He's such a hottie! I mean, really. Though that Boy Scout honor is a little downer for me anyway."

I push her playfully. "Stop. You're not dating him."

Emily applies her makeup setting spray, whatever

the heck that is, and smiles. "Yes, true. Well, it seems like he makes you happy. Do tell me more. I love hearing about it all." She moves me so that I'm no longer facing the mirror and begins to apply primer to my eyelids. "Seriously, spill."

"I really like him a lot. It's just . . . that whole blood vow and Guardian thing. Like, I'd like him to just be a guy at school."

"Will, may I remind you that he is a guy at school."

"No, that's not what I mean," I laugh. "It's this veil that hangs over my mind. Because of this blood vow he made to my father, I'm not completely certain his intentions are his decision rather than something he's compelled to do."

Emily moves quickly over my eyebrows, then she's back at my lids with small brushes. "Just because a vow uniquely connects you doesn't mean his brain is mush and under some ultimate control. His decisions are his own, Will."

But are they?

"Another thing. Stop trying to find a reason that he can't like you as much as you like him. Don't sabotage it by pushing people away. You don't have to be some martyr of a Queen either."

She really knows me and how to nail what I'm thinking, and we don't even have a vow, just our friendship. She's totally right. I pout for Emily as she applies lip gloss to my lips.

"You are my masterpiece!" Emily announces at last.

I'm stunned when I see myself. Highlights and delicate glitter showcase my cheekbones, and there are yellow and burnt orange shadows on my eyes. I never do much besides a colored face lotion, mascara, and lip gloss.

"Speak, Will, speak!"

I pull pearl drop dangle earrings through my ears. "Wow, Emily. Thank you. I could be a model at a photo shoot."

Emily puts on her black lacy dress and finishes tying on her bright red high tops. She looks glamorous in her own spunky, styled way.

Eoin knocks and opens the door. "Are you ladies ready?"

CHAPTER 21

I stop at the end of the hall and look down the stairs. Rhydian is waiting for me in the foyer, gorgeous in a formal black and white tuxedo, his dark wavy locks styled. I spot the leather wrist cuff, and the glinting silver of the earpiece clipped on the ridge of his ear. He's forever a Guardian, and right now, he's all mine. My heart beats loudly in my chest. Emily is right; I'm head over heels for him, and he didn't even have to do any of the small things like the fairies at the lake, the dinners, the hugs, the kissing, the moments of pure comfort.

Eoin clears his throat and, finally, Rhydian looks from Emily and Cross up the staircase to me. His immediate smile reveals his dimple.

At the bottom of the stairs, I turn, and the skirt spins out from my waist in a beautiful canopy of folds that stretch in a tulip shape around me. "So, Quinn and Emily did well?"

"I'd say they had a beautiful subject for whom they only accentuated what was already there."

I hope I'm not turning beet red.

Rhydian slowly reaches for my wrist and places a beautiful silver and white rose corsage on me. "This is customary, right?"

I smile in response and touch the roses. "Yes. This is beautiful. Thank you." My skin tingles at the touch of his hand on mine. The silver elastic band of the corsage has small knots tied in it. I smile at him and rub one of the tiny balled knots. "So, more knot magick. What do you wish for?"

He whispers in my ear, "A few slow dances with you." I close my eyes, feeling his body so close to mine, and I wish for the same thing.

I faintly hear Cross ask, "Are ya both ready?"

They're talking, but I don't hear them. I'm caught up in Rhydian's presence. He holds my hand and leads me to the front door, where Eoin stops us.

"Wait, let me get a few pictures before you leave." He snaps a few pictures of us at the door with my phone, and I put it back in my clutch. Rhydian kisses my forehead lightly. When we walk outside, I see what was supposed to be a limo but looks more like a HUMV with an extended back end.

Cross laughs out loud and claps his hands together. "Excellent!"

Tullen waves to us and opens the passenger side door. "Shall we?"

Emily smiles. "Yes, we shall!"

Cross helps Emily into the vehicle. He looks

younger when he smiles. Emily mirrors him, and they look good together.

"May I?" Tullen asks, his hand outstretched to assist me into the HUMV. I gather my skirt in my other hand and use a hidden step to enter.

Inside, I slide over and find Cross and Emily on opposite sides of bench seats laughing and opening a bottle. Emily plays with the ceiling lights overhead and the volume of music coming through the speakers.

Rhydian slides in next to me.

"This is quite the tank," I say.

"Oh, you have no idea," he says. "I think Eoin would have preferred a tank. I'm surprised Tullen and Quinn were not able to secure one." I giggle and snuggling into his warm shoulder.

The ride to prom is nice. The car is warm, and I like how Rhydian's eyes keep gravitating to mine. I want to kiss him, and I can sense that he wants the same thing. The only thing keeping us apart is Emily and Cross laughing and joking in the car, though they didn't seem to pay us much attention.

When we get to the hotel, Rhydian and Cross exit first, then help Emily and me out of the car. A red carpet leads us into the fancy hotel as if we are arriving at some big awards ceremony. We are late as planned, and I can only stay for a short time, but I'll take it.

Interlinking my arm with Rhydian's, I lean against him and walk into the lobby. The hotel is resplendent with marble floors and crystal chandeliers that lead toward the check-in desk. Some signs and balloons direct us to the Trinity Cross Senior Prom.

Cross and Emily's matching Converse squeak against the clean floor.

"It's like we're following ducks with all that noise they're making."

I grin. "I'm surprised there's not a fountain full of swans with this hotel's high caliber."

The pathway pivots around the lobby's back wall, and a four-tier fountain comes into view. A gentle flow of water cascades from the fountain's peak into the larger body of water that is illuminated in jewel-colored tones.

"Wow, you called it. The swans must be in their beds asleep at this hour."

The archway we approach leads to two sets of double doors decorated by a white and black balloon arch. The music and noise coming from the room is loud. Now that we're here, I can hardly believe we've made it to the dance.

There are two security guards stationed outside the doors—Guardians with clipboards.

"Name?"

Cross laughs as Emily gives her name. When the younger Guardian waits for Cross to respond, Cross reaches behind his head and smacks it. "I'm her guest, ya dim wit."

Rhydian and I approach the other Guardian, who seems nervous. He says in a low whisper, "A pleasure, your grace." The veil of being a typical teen at prom was never going to be a solid one anyway. Even here I reign the Wiccan Queen at her senior prom.

I nod to him. "Thank you." Rhydian leads us through the balloon arch to the dance.

The ballroom is high class. Coral's family spared no expense on the decorations, flowers, or buffet with finger foods and drinks. The front is a staging area with two huge screens that flash pictures and videos while the DJ operates the music. Round tables are scattered to the left and right sides of a large dance floor.

"Let's go to the left."

We follow Emily and Cross, passing a photo op wall for students to take pictures at. Everyone is smiling and dancing. I spy Marco laughing across the room with several of his friends from the football team.

"Are you hungry or thirsty? Would you like anything?"

"Maybe a drink?"

Rhydian pulls out a chair for me, and Emily and I sit at the empty table with little tea lights glowing around a flower centerpiece of white, black, and gold.

"Wow, can you believe it? Prom, Will."

"It's more than I imagined it would be. It's surreal. I didn't go to prom last year. I wasn't sure what to expect."

Emily's smile is prominent as she watches Cross.

"So, did you work out the stuff in your head about Rhy?"

"I'm the girl in the moment."

"That's my girl." She touches my shoulder and looks in my eyes before standing as Cross and Rhydian return to the table.

"These are foo-foo alcohol-free drinks." Cross hands Emily a pink cocktail. "But they are pretty tasty."

My drink looks almost holographic with opulent colors in the clear liquid.

"What is this?" I ask

"They call it lovers lane, so I took a chance."

His eyes are on my lips. I take a sip, watching him watch me. I don't feel nervous, just at ease.

The drink is refreshing. It has a slight taste of coconut and smells of vanilla and rose. It's like spa water, but the color and ice give it the effect of something more.

"And?"

"Quite refreshing. Would you like to try?"

The music changes from a slower tempo to a thumping beat.

"Yes! Let's goooooo." Emily and Cross make their way to the dance floor, and we follow.

The music is thundering. I gather my long skirt up in one hand and swing my hips as Emily jumps up and down. Cross and Rhydian move with us. Cross's jumping with his thick brown arms over his head pulls his shirt out of his slacks. A second song continues with the same pumping beat, and the sheen on everyone starts to show.

Rhydian says something, but all I can recognize is my name on his lips.

"What?" I yell back, and as I move closer to find out what he said, a kiss lands on my lips and stops everything. His hands are at my waist, pulling me closer to him. The crowd of bodies on the dance floor fades away. I only know him, his breath, his lips, and tongue. I breathe his name and smile when he pulls back from me. He grins.

"Wow. You're so happy and beautiful, I couldn't resist any longer."

My heart is beating fast in time with the music. We stand still as everyone around us moves. I lean up to Rhydian and kiss him gently as the beat changes, and we are holding each other to the slower tempo.

Those around us move, and space opens for couples. My face almost hurts from smiling. I put my head on his shoulder with our bodies pressed together, dancing. This feels so good. His hand is on my lower back, the other holding my hand tucked to his chest.

"Willow?"

"Yeah?"

"This is good, Willow. It really is."

He says what I'm feeling, and the confirmation doesn't make me nervous or flush. It seals worry away with an agreement. This is his choice. I'm his choice.

The song ends, and the lights change. I spy Daniel dancing with Lucy. They are not far away, but the idea of them is. The normal that I want fades into the light.

There is a disruption in the music with a mic tap from headmaster Ms. Chin.

"Seniors, please come together with me in thanking our benefactors for this event, Mr. and Mrs. Yang."

A light shines on Coral's parents. Her father is distinguished in his custom-fitted suit. There is some gray in the hairline near his temples. Her mother looks not much older than Coral herself. She is not of Asian heritage, which surprises me. Coral stands near her father with a wide but not authentic smile.

"I also have the honor of announcing your prom court. The votes are in and tallied to represent the prom court tonight. Your prom king is . . ." Ms. Chin opens a large white envelope. "Steve Carlin!"

Several girls wipe at their eyes, and few guys near us clap as Steve approaches the stage with a cane.

"Thank you for this honor. I'm glad to be out of the hospital and, of course, looking forward to the afterparty." Everyone cheers. Rhydian squeezes my hand, and I squeeze back. I will be back in Edayri; no afterparties for me.

As the noise drops, Ms. Chin continues. "And now for your prom queen . . ." She opens a second white envelope and announces, "Coral Yang!"

"No way any of that is a coincidence," Emily whispers to me.

"Who cares, really." I smile and clap with everyone.

"Come on, Will, where is your sense of justice? Rebecca or Shelly would have been better choices."

"Because wearing a plastic crown is the pentacle of achievement? Let her have it. Who cares." Emily wiggles her eyebrows and laughs mockingly. All I can do is shake my head and grin. I doubt Ms. Chin was surprised by these white envelopes. It's appropriate for Steve and for Coral, as much as it would have pained me to think kindly of Coral in a friendly way before. The weight of old grudges has no place in my thoughts tonight.

The dance floor parts and Steve leads Coral to the center, where they sway to the Post Malone song "Circles." Coral's parents watching with smiles while talking and shaking hands with Ms. Chin. My attention is taken by hands on my waist turning me, and I look into Rhydian's hazel, green-blue eyes. I lay my head on his shoulder, and we sway through the songs. I lose track of time, and the changing music blends into one blissful moment.

"Are you having a good time?"

"I am. Are you? Having a good time?"

"Anytime with you is good." He glances behind me. "Let's go sit for a bit."

We walk to the table where Emily and Cross are chatting with Marco and his date, and I realize the ballroom is bare for the first time. Less than twenty students remain.

The lights flicker, signaling the end of the night. It's been a full hour since we arrived.

Lucy taps me on the shoulder and gives me a hug. "Hey, you look beautiful!"

"Thanks! So do you," I say in return. Daniel and Rhydian stand next to each other awkwardly.

"You've been dancing all night. Are you going to

the afterparty? There are two different options, which is kinda awesome." Lucy says.

"No, I think we have to go. I was pushing it for the time I was here, I don't want to tempt fate further." I look over my shoulder at Rhydian. He turns with his hand to his earpiece, speaking low. Cross's face is all business when he approaches Rhydian and the air in the room shifts. The night is over—my stomach sinks.

"There is an issue outside. Cross, check-in with Tullen. I need to check in with Eoin at the house." Rhydian looks at me. "You and Emily stay here." There is no worry in his voice with the simple request.

The lights flicker overhead, and the hotel staff come in and begin to break down tables. The ambiance of the ballroom changes from a swanky room filled with formally dressed teenagers to just a place. The balloons and decor are removed from view. Rhydian transports to Eoin, and I hug my stomach, awaiting the news.

"So, which party should we all go to?" Emily asks.

Daniel pulls me into their conversation, "Willow, will you be coming too?"

"Sure. Maybe." I shrug my shoulders. It's not on the agenda, and I don't want to push my luck. I don't want this night to end, but maybe it wouldn't have to end with Rhydian. Am I hoping for a more intimate situation with him?

"Coral invited us to Steve's parents' lake house. It is farther away, but it could be fun," Lucy says with a lilt to her voice. Emily's face scrunches up at Coral's name.

"How about the party right here, in the hotel rooms on the eighth floor? There is a whole suite of rooms on that floor. We could just hang here. Let's at least check it out." Emily says.

We agree and move toward the double doors. They slam shut, and the lights flicker again. The screech that reaches my ears is unbearable. The sound vibrates and shakes the entire room, bringing us all to our knees. A dark mist shapes itself into corporal forms draped in tattered robes, and they swarm the ballroom. Phantoms.

Emily pushes Lucy and me behind the catering table to obscure us from view. Daniel runs toward the closest door and tries to open it, but the door doesn't move. He rushes back to us.

The screams of the staff all but drown out the high screeching sound. There is a light behind the DJ stage—a door. I watch the hotel staff escape. "Em, look over there. An escape, but it's on the other side."

Lucy's eyes are wide, and tears threaten to fall. Her shoulders are shaking. Daniel's eyes are full of fear too, but he takes off his coat and pulls it around her.

"That's too far—"

"We feel you. You belong to us. You will free us." The phantom voices are clear and many.

Lucy's eyes beg Emily in a plea for help. I kick off my high heel shoes. There is only one way out; we will need to fight. They are after Lucy, and I will not let that happen. My magick hums and swirls on my skin at my command. I know my crown is showing because my vision has a hazy glowing sheen right above it.

I pull Emily's attention to me. "Only one way out." She nods in agreement. Daniel stares at me, mouth slack, while loosely pulling Lucy into the crook of his arm.

"See if you can reach Rhydian through the blood vow thing," Emily says.

I close my eyes, focus, and reach out to him, but there is nothing.

"Rhydian, we're under attack. The phantoms—"

Bang!

The double doors crack loudly, and I hear yelling outside. Emily smiles and says, "It's Cross."

The door busts at its hinges and flies over tables and chairs. Cross is in full Guardian armor, bulked and ready to fight. We all move toward the opening he's made.

A mist forms around me when I stand and instant pain elicits my scream. There are screams all around me, too. Then I'm thrown. I'm flying away from the door, still screaming. I tuck my head before hitting hard into tables and chairs. I'm a tangle of dress, chair legs, and limbs when I finally stop moving.

"Em! Willow!" Cross's voice booms.

I see him fighting figures in the mist around him, ducking and turning, his massive sword connecting with a semi-corporal form. There is the blur of another phantom behind him with more fog. I tug at my dress. I'm pinned. I pull and feel my magick fading. There is blood from cuts on my arms and legs. Pain shoots up my right leg as I come free.

Fuck!

"Willow, use your magick!"

Emily is in her full valkyrie battle gear on the opposite side of the ballroom, swinging her staff and surrounded by mist.

I try to stand but fall to my knees when my ankle collapses under me. The throbbing sensation of fire makes me shudder. I call to my magick and place my hands on it.

"Mend the broken and torn—"

The mist is around me suddenly. It yanks me high in the air, but I push my own magick at the fog and drop, landing on my toes and not falling flat on my face. My ankle screams in pain, and I roll. My skirt is torn. Cursing, I magick it away and replace it with leggings.

Emily pounds her staff on the floor. The shock wave clears the mist from the ground up to the roof, and Cross is at my side.

"Heal it, now!"

I reach for my ankle, but Cross yanks my hand to his bloody side.

The roar of a tiger echoes through more screams.

I mutter the spell to myself. I feel his lungs fill with air, his muscles repair themselves in knitting fashion as his skin molds back. My hands are slick with Cross's dark blood.

The humming grows dull. My magick is fading on me.

I push through a veil in myself to hold onto the hum, the magick, the unwanted part of myself that is now who I am, who I'm meant to be.

Cross pats my hand. "Thank ya."

He's healed.

Emily is shaking; the bubble she formed is only around the three of us. Marco is in his tiger form chasing a phantom away from the few classmates and hotel staff in the ballroom.

"Where is—"

"Tullen, Rhydian, Quinn—all unreachable. Something is wrong." Frustrated, Cross holds his broken ear cuff.

"My magick isn't—"

"Fight anyway." Cross hands me a dagger. "The mist is a diversion from their bodies. Find the soft spots, don't let them connect with you, then do some fuckin' damage. They bleed and can be killed."

I stand, favoring my weight to the side opposite my injured ankle. My back to Cross, I take my defensive stance.

My body shakes. This isn't training anymore.

"I can't . . . hold . . ." Emily's stance is wavering, the mist pushing at the bubble, the screams and shrieks piercing.

"Don't. Let 'em come!" Cross yells.

The rush is immediate. The mist surrounds us, and the pain cuts all over me. I thrash out with the dagger and move. The mist follows the movement. It can't stay on me; I can't handle the pain. I duck and roll to the ground, calling my magick to surround me and protect my skin. Popping up, I stand and thrust the dagger forward. It connects with something substantial, and I push forward to sink then twist the blade. Something howls and hits my face, knocking me back, and the dagger is lost from my grip. The dagger looks suspended until the phantom appears, corpse-like hands pulling at the hilt.

I run toward it, jump, and connect my elbow to its head. Grabbing the hilt, I yank the dagger out and slice hard where my elbow hit—the shrieking stops. The phantom falls to the floor and dissolves away in its mist.

The agonized screaming continues around me. My friends.

Cross runs toward me, the mist behind him growing. He's yelling, one hand up to his wrist cuff. His face is stone and determined. He cups his hand in front of him, and I know what he wants me to do. I run toward him, dagger in hand, swinging my arms hard. He leans down, and when I put my foot in his hand, I soar high above him, swinging the dagger down from above my head and connecting with another phantom.

Landing hard, my ankle buckles. Cross is next to me.

"One left. They got this. I need to transport you out—"

Emily and Lucy get thrown. Daniel grabs her staff and swings it, but the phantom's arm goes right through his stomach.

Time turns to slow motion. The sounds are gone from my head. I watch Daniel fall to the floor. I yank my arm from Cross and transport to Daniel. The mist surrounds me, pushing. I swing the dagger, connecting and slicing, moving in a dance of rolling, ducking, swinging. Pain is all around me, all through my body and mind. I hear myself screaming.

Kill. Save him.

I'm glowing. My magick finds the phantom and twists it. The shrieks and howls match my yells until it dissolves in front of Daniel and me.

"Willow?"

I turn to Cross, blade raised. His hands are up in surrender.

Not a threat.

"Willow! Oh my God, help him!" Lucy screams behind me.

"The phantoms are gone, for now," Cross says, his arms slowly dropping to his side.

Turning, I survey the damage. Dark blood pools around Daniel. His stomach is dark and gaping, a hole right through him. His arm is at an unnatural angle, his face pale, his eyes staring off in the distance.

He is gone.

My mind, my body, goes numb.

Death follows me.

Lucy and Emily are yelling at each other, Emily holding Lucy back. I'm a spectator. Cross's lips are moving, but I can't understand him.

My magick leaves me.

Lucy and Emily's voices fade.

I couldn't save him. He is gone.

Lucy pulls Daniel to her.

"You can't do this!" Emily yells. "You don't know what you're doing!"

My voice breaks free of my mind, and I hear myself say, "He wouldn't choose this."

"He'd choose to be alive!"

"No, Lucy. Not like that," Marco says.

"AAAAH!" Her scream rebounds around us, chilling my blood.

Lucy is glowing and encasing herself with Daniel. I can't help the streaming tears and anguish that push me to the floor in a heap of emotion.

A tiger's roar echoes through the ballroom.

PART IV

By knot of eight, it will be fate
By knot of nine, what's done is mine

I'm watching the same events unfold. First Mrs. Scott, then my father, and now Daniel. It's as if I'm watching television without the sound. I see it all unfolding, but I can't completely comprehend. Daniel is no longer here. His body is present, his eyes unmoving, his face stone. There is nothing left to do.

Death the one constant you can count on in the end. I tried to protect my friends and failed. I wanted to attend prom. Was I the impetus that brought the phantoms here? Was it Lucy? Does it even matter?

She's mumbling and chanting, her hands moving over Daniel in weird patterns and waves. I call to my magick, but the familiar hum is gone. I'm an empty shell on autopilot. Looking around, I find Cross surveying the room. We need to move. It's not safe here.

"What are you doing? You dismiss who you are, then draw from a force you don't respect or understand. You've heard everyone! He wouldn't want this. Stop what you are doing!" Emily yells at Lucy.

Marco paces in tiger form on the other side of me, his pads soft on the ground. He's keeping watch as well.

Emily holds her hands up in surrender when Lucy continues her chant, then carefully slides next to Lucy. Em stares at Daniel, expressionless. They chant together and emanate a glow all around Daniel's body. When Emily moves her hand over his stomach, Daniel's chest rises awkwardly, and something cracks loudly. A bone-breaking or mending? Lucy gasps at the sound, but Emily shoves her shoulder into her, still concentrating, and they continue. His body starts to respond by contracting inward like a pulse.

They are making him an einherjar warrior.

This is part of Norse culture that Emily told me about—bringing dead warriors back in service to the valkyrie. Not all dead warriors take to the magical calling from the valkyrie, so this may do nothing.

As if I'm speaking to Daniel, I contemplate the questions in my head. Did you want to be a soldier in service to the valkyrie and Lucy?

I shake my head hard. What am I thinking! If he could come back, he should, right? What wouldn't I give to have my father and Mrs. Scott back? Is it selfish to want them all back, to want Daniel again, to feel like I didn't fail?

Cross approaches. I pull myself up and stand next to him.

"My magick is gone."

"How do ya know? Ya may have just used all that ye had. Maybe ya need time to recover."

"That's never been the issue before." Maybe I've done something wrong by the Goddess?

Cross points to Emily and Lucy, who continue to chant around Daniel. "No kidding." He shakes his head. "Tullen wasn't near the car, and I can't reach any of the Guardians. We are on our own. Feels like a setup."

The pallor of Daniel's skin is coming back to life. He turns his head and looks directly at me. His eyes are cloudy; this isn't quite Daniel. Lucy stops chanting. Emily moves quickly as Daniel jumps to his feet and crouches in a fighter stance at a speed I can barely track with my eyes. Cross throws his arms in front of me and yanks me behind him. Lucy, on the floor closest to Daniel, gasps when he snarls at her. Marco crawls between Daniel and us.

Daniel scans the room. His eyes stop on me. His head tilts like a bird's; he recognizes me. Lucy reaches her hand toward him, but he doesn't seem to understand. His mouth opens without a sound, but his face says it all—agony and rage. Tears well in my eyes and my shoulders quake.

"Daniel," I whisper, and his face turns to look at me through Cross and Marco.

In one quick movement, Cross turns to me and transports me to the door of the ballroom. I waiver on my feet. Daniel is running and leaping toward us with Marco trailing.

I've lost sight of Emily and Lucy. Cross puts me

behind him. Daniel halts his speed just before Cross and swings his hips in a roundhouse kick that connects with Cross's face, pushing him to the floor. The power and strength to move Cross like that is more than what Daniel had before.

Marco transforms back to his human form and holds his hand out in surrender. "Daniel, buddy, what are you doing? Do you need to protect her?"

Daniel nods in a small, quick, awkward movement.

My voice shakes. "I'm safe. Cross is my Guardian. We are all safe, okay?"

He straightens and moves toward me, tentatively as if he doesn't want to spook me. I'm totally spooked. This is Daniel, but not.

"Can you talk?"

He opens his mouth as if testing the function. "Yes." His voice is low and deep, but it's still Daniel's voice.

"Daniel!"

Lucy and Emily come up behind him too fast. He turns toward them and snarls in warning, protecting me again. I'm close to him, and I reach my hand forward. Marco and Cross protest behind me, but I ignore them and touch Daniel's shoulder.

He relaxes.

"It's okay. Those are our friends, Lucy and Emily."

Lucy repeats his name, but he continues to stare at me, his eyes searching for an answer from me.

"What is wrong with him? Daniel, it's me, Lucy. Your girlfriend."

Daniel watches her but makes no response, then

looks back at me. He steps closer to me, reaches up, and touches my face. His hand is cold and stiff.

He's here.

I reach my hand out to Lucy, and she puts her hand in mine. I bring her closer to Daniel. His eyes shift between Lucy and me. "Lucy. Daniel, do you remember Lucy?"

Her eyes are wide and searching his face, almost pleading. This is heartbreaking. She is crumbling in front of everyone.

"Daniel." Emily's commanding voice orders him. "Fall in line."

He moves swiftly behind Emily, who looks like a supernatural general in her filigree eagle headdress and brass armor that has replaced her ruined dress.

"What are you doing?" Lucy's voice waivers.

"This is what you've made him. He's a solider. He will protect the Queen as that is what I've sworn to do. As a valkyrie, you've made no declaration, Lucy. If you want to be in his life, you'll need to make the declaration."

"No. No." Lucy pulls away from me. It's a rejection that I wasn't expecting to hurt so strongly. I think about Evan and his story about the Horned God and the Goddess, their rejection and anger. Lucy throws her hands in the air. "This? Look around, Willow. This is what you've brought—you and Emily! We almost died."

"If not for the friends yer rejecting, you would have. Ungrateful," Cross spits.

I give him a warning look. She's not entirely wrong.

Emily laughs hysterically. Marco is standing behind her with Daniel. "No, Lucy, this is what *you* brought, what *you* did to Daniel. Play victim though! That's a role you've got down. Make a mess and take no responsibility for it."

"Fuck you!" Lucy is shaking.

Cross pulls my attention away. "This is their family matter. Let's transport—"

Boom!

Crack!

Evan transports a few feet opposite Cross and me with Theon and one other. The vibration pushes me back a step and awakens the pain in my ankle.

"We've got to go," Evan says.

Lucy is staring daggers at me as if I'm responsible for Daniel and Cross, putting themselves between Evan and me.

I want to experience sadness for her, but right now, all I feel is her jealousy.

"Now, Willow! Everyone grabs a hand." Evan yells.

Cross grabs mine, and when Daniel reaches for me, I pull away. "Emily, Marco, take them somewhere else. We need to split up."

The ballroom lights flicker, and the temperature drops. Phantoms are coming.

This is officially the prom from hell.

CHAPTER 24

The push and pull of the transport magick is anything but smooth. My magick usually steadies and helps with transporting. Now my eyes can't track from the motion of being jerked around, and I try to hold down my stomach, knowing if I don't, I will vomit all over Cross and Evan. When we stop, vertigo overtakes me. I bend over and throw up on the ground.

Evan is next to me, patting my back in weird circles, and I stand.

"Where are—" I cut myself off when I see the overturned logs and blazing fire surrounded by tents. We are in the same place the demon teenagers took me. Theon walks away from us giving orders that I can't make out.

"What the hell is going on, Evan?"

We are in the heart of the Emissaries camp. Cross has moved off to the side and is talking to General Thaxam and Abby, leaving me with Evan. Ax smiles his fang tooth grin and shrugs his boxy red shoulders. It's like watching the devil try to put me at ease. Still, the menacing horns and exterior are anything but innocent.

"It's complicated," Evan says.

"Seriously! We are well beyond complicated!" I scream at him. "Phantoms were at my prom! They killed Daniel! And where is Rhydian, Quinn, and Tullen?" The tones of conversation around me pause, and all eyes are on us.

"Prom," he says as if testing the word on his tongue. "Around and around we go, the dancing does continue."

"What does that mean? Evan, no riddles! I need you to fully pull it together."

"I am always fully together. Are you questioning my sanity?" The looks around us catch my anger in my throat.

"I'm sorry, Evan. Truly, I am," I say in defeat.

"I'm not. It was a catalyst of change for something much more."

I turn to Ax and Abby. "Tell me now."

Ax begins to talk, Abby filling in his pauses. "Phantoms are emerging from the fountain in the center of the Hallowed Hall. The Guardians are supposed to be containing the threat but—"

"But the Guardians have been taken over by some sort of spell and are fighting any who resist."

"It's a genocide, Willow. They are wiping out anyone who fights back. There seems to be some type of gateway in at the manor. It's an all-out clash of

Edayri. The phantoms scream for you, Willow. There is something they need to complete the task. We think they are attempting to permanently connect the fallen Norse realm to Edayri. A Convergence."

"Meaning the destabilization of Edayri as well," Abby finishes.

"So, we must keep ya here, away from all of it," Cross says.

"We can't do that. How will we ever win? She has the strongest magick. Everyone in our family is strong, but she's the most," Evan says. The absence of a hum makes me flinch at Evan's words. I have nothing to help. Also, what about everyone else? This is horrible.

"Evan, we need to know what we are walking into," Abby replies.

"The Guardians. Does that mean that—Rhydian is at the manor?" I start to shake. "Abby?"

She shakes her head. "We're working a plan of interception to move out those that are hurt and—"

Evan dramatically closes and opens his eyes, inhaling sharply. "He's there."

"What? Are you sure?" I ask. I'm ready to leave and find him, but I can't transport without magick or a plan. I need others to help me get to him.

"If Evan had a vision, then yes, Rhydian is there," Theon says, surprising me as he comes up from behind Ax.

I stumble back, and the weight makes my ankle smart again.

"Are you hurt?" Abby looks at my ankle. Before I

can move, she places her hand on my foot. It warms to her touch.

"Abby, what are you doing?"

"She's a healer," Cross says. "Ya need to be in top form. We've got to go to MacKinnon Manor. Eoin has reached out." Cross taps his Guardian wrist cuff. "He and a small contingency group are trying to contain the phantoms from wreaking havoc all over Edayri. They have closed the Hallowed Hall, and the focus now seems to be at the manor. This could be where the control is—whoever released them."

"Just a minute, Cross. Willow, follow me."

I follow Abby to a tent. Looking around the small space, it feels more like a bedroom than a tent for camping. There is a full bed at the back wall with a nightstand and lamps, a dresser off to the side, and a small table with two chairs in the center. Rugs cover the floor.

Abby hands me a pair of boots. I quickly pull on and lace them. I had forgotten I was barefoot until she healed my ankle. I catch sight of myself in a standing mirror opposite, dressed in leggings and the bodice that my ruined prom dress has been reduced to. I gesture to a dark shirt with a hood lying on the table and, when she nods, I pull it on.

"Do you need anything else?" Abby asks.

"No. Thank you for this." Looking at her, I see Rhydian's resemblance in her dark hair and the shape of her nose and mouth. Their eyes are different, his a dark stormy ocean with blues and greens while Abby's are dark brown. I finger what's left of the corsage on my wrist and touch one of the small knots of the silver band.

"Do you live here? Does your father—"

"I don't live here full time, but I'm here a lot. He knows nothing. Neither does Rhydian, but I'm guessing it will come out soon." She looks at her hands. "I never betrayed your intentions of an Edayri governing body, the legion council."

"I never thought you did," I say quickly.

"I think what the Emissaries stand for is exactly what you're putting in place, so coordinating allows me to weave the two together."

"I see that."

The relief on her face is surprising. Abby gets up to leave, and I tell her I'll be a minute. I call to my magick, but there's nothing—no hum, no tingle, no awareness of anything lingering.

Can I call to Rhydian? I focus on the quiet of the tent and reach out through my mind, thinking of his handsome face when I came down the stairs in my dress just several hours ago before prom.

"Rhydian." I breathe.

Silence answers me.

I open my eyes and take a deep breath before opening Abby's tent's flap to leave.

"Willow, come find me. I'm hurt."

Rhydian. I hear him clearly in my head. He's guiding me to him, the outreach pulling at my mind and my body. This is a tether to me, to my whole being. Where is he?

Evan grabs my arm. "You're not going to him

without us. It's a trap, Willow." Evan closes his eyes before he says, "He's at the manor."

"Trap or not, I have to go." My voice is almost pleading.

"Yes, you do, but with us in tow." His hold on my arm is gentle, and everyone—Cross, Abby, Ax, Evan, Theon, and other demons—reaches out and touches someone else in the group.

"I don't want to ask this of you, coming into battle, but I thank you and—be careful," I say

"In your name, Blessed Be," Abby says as a prayer.

Cross guides us in the transport. Evan keeps his hand gentle on mine as Cross leads us onto the grounds of MacKinnon Manor, my new home.

The realization comes to me the moment Evan releases my arm.

This is a bad idea.

CHAPTER 25

We are hidden on the side of the property where the tree line begins. The fighting is chaos, armored Guardians fighting against other Guardians and Wiccans fighting Wiccans. Phantoms screech and charge through a group of demons at the side of the MacKinnon Manor. They all fall flat on the ground, unmoving. I can't tell who is fighting who; it's just a swarm of magick, swords, punches, and blood.

So much blood.

The Emissaries around me are organizing and entering the fight. I can't move. I envision my father flat on the ground, dead, not far from where I stand. His body is bloodied and broken from the torture imposed on him to get his power and lure me in for mine. This is, once again, the goal.

I block out the image and stare at my hands, flexing them and calling to my magick. A faint light shows at the tips of my fingers. I'm limited, but is it coming back?

The longer I watch, the easier I recognize who is being controlled and who isn't. The noble covens are fighting with the rogue Guardians under some type of spell, their movements mechanical. It looks all wrong.

Cross is next to me. "Don't go all hero. Be smart and use yer training, mind, and body. Yer a warrior; ya don't need to rely on magick. Get blasted mad, woman!" he yells.

I smirk at the compliment from Cross. He just called me a warrior, and I can't help but stand a little straighter despite being scared.

"Ya fight best when yer pissed off at me. Do I need to tell ya something offensive?" I shake my head. "Fuckin' tear it up. Don't over complicate this; find Eoin and end this spell. Pocket that other shit. Let's go."

"Eoin's there!" Evan points.

Following his gesture, I can barely make out Eoin on the front entry stairs, but I recognize it's him by his armor with golden shoulders.

"Rhydian!" Abby screams.

I follow her to where she is looking and find him. The armor covering his body has dark blood smeared all over it. His movements are fluid and undeterred as he cuts through those in front of him. He brings his sword down and slices through two magical beings while behind him, a phantom protects his blindside.

They are working together.

Rhydian's face is mechanical, zombie-like with everyone around him. His eyes, dispassionate, focus on Abby and then shift to me, his target.

His mouth is moving, but it's too loud for me to hear him. I step out of the tree line as a demon crosses in front of Rhydian, distracting him.

Evan grabs my hand, and we transport too Eoin. Evan places a protective magickal bubble around the three of us. I gasp. Eoin has burn marks on one side of his face and scorches down the side of his body.

Evan places his hand on Eoin and begins healing him. "Sabine? Is she here?" Evan spits Sabine's name like a sour lemon.

"Yes. I narrowly escaped control." He shows his palm with a specific mark of protection that glows like lava in his skin. "The Guardians have been taken over by a spell, and only severe pain and fire of high magick is releasing it. I'm not sure how long it will last." Eoin starts to cough. "The phantoms are guarding the manor. Someone is letting them in. They are collapsing the bridge between realms. The only way to do that is to siphon your powers." He reaches for my hand, "Once you are drained—I don't know what's next."

My heart beats faster knowing it's someone else doing this. Why did I think something was wrong with me? The Goddess crown me, but the royal powers are also mine, along with my own and my father's. I had the notion deep down that the Goddess could take away magick as easily as she gave it, perhaps as a punishment for Daniel. But she wouldn't take my powers like this.

"This doesn't seem like an unsolvable puzzle, then," Evan says. "Where is the source of the siphon?"

"From what I can tell, it must be in the house, in the lower basements."

The dungeons. That was where father and Lucy were held before the rescue.

I hear Cross's familiar battle cry muffled behind us. Rhydian must be near.

Evan pulls his hand from Eoin, and we are no longer in a bubble. The sound of the battle is at full volume. I flinch.

"Sabine." Evan takes off running.

Sabine stands ahead of him and to the side of where a Guardian lays motionless. Her purple cloak billows behind her movements, her brilliant red hair like a flame fanned out around her. I can't see who she is fighting; is she fighting with the Guardians or against others? The phantoms are concentrated near the lower end of the manor and are moving her direction.

Sabine conjures a hard blow to a massive demon that knocks him down at Evan's feet.

The distance closes between Sabine and Evan.

My breath is gone. I can't do anything to stop it.

Evan has a light ball in his hands and throws it at Sabine, blasting her with a direct hit. She falls in a heap on the ground. Evan turns and throws a light ball at Quinn, who is running at him fast.

Did he kill her? My feet move of their own accord toward the purple cloak.

"Sabine. Sabine." I shake her, and the grimace is immediate. Her shirt is burned, and the mark on her shoulder is like Eoin's. Evan woke her from the trance of the spell controlling her. He didn't kill her.

"Willow." Sabine is no longer under someone else's control. She pulls at her ear and holds out an earpiece that I've only seen on Guardians. Grabbing a rock, she crushes it.

"It's how they control them, us—"

"Evan!" I yell. He's a good twenty feet away from us. "The earpieces! That is how the Guardians are being controlled."

Evan and Quinn are exchanging blows. Evan grabs his neck, pulls the earpiece off his ear, then drops Quinn. Quinn sees me and stops with his eyebrows raised. He seems to understand quickly and immediately transports to Eoin. They fight in tandem against others at the entrance.

The battle is closing in on us.

Rhydian is closer to me now. His face is unfeeling. I recognize his calculation, his determination. He won't kill me, but he will hurt me, subdue me—it's the order.

Bring her by any means necessary. I hear it in my head like an echo from Rhydian.

"Rhydian, no!" Abby hits his back with a magick light ball. It covers his armor but does nothing. He stalks forward, matching my steps as I step backward. He uses his magick to throw Sabine into Evan.

If I turn and run, I won't be able to track him, and I'll get caught. He'll use magick. I must keep this physical; otherwise, I won't have a chance. Unless . . . Maybe

I can overpower the spell by using his loyalty to our bond. Isn't that what he told me before? He couldn't hurt me unless I allowed it, and it would tear our bond.

"Rhydian." I hold out my hand, and he stops advancing. "Your vow. Do you remember what you vowed to my father and pledged to me?"

His eyes wander around me, no longer focused.

Eoin yells from behind me. "Follow your Queen, Rhydian. Protect what you vowed—"

I'm thrown back, and I hit the manor's stone wall hard. I expect pain when I fall, but I'm cushioned with air before I hit the ground. Eoin is stopping my decent, his hand outreached to me.

Rhydian pushes himself up from the ground and throws a dagger at Eoin, who catches it in his hand and throws it back at him. Still, it's too late. Rhydian and Evan both run toward me as I try to stand.

Rhydian slams into me and we are transporting before I have time to think. I reach for Evan, my hand just shy of his fingertips. Everything blurs. Rhydian pulls me into his chest, and we land hard on a dirt floor.

CHAPTER 26

Breath escapes my lungs at the force of impact. I moan through the pain and push myself up. Rhydian is next to me and I crawl away, frantically trying to get out of his grip. I roll on the dirt floor and try to gain traction with my feet as I kick him in the stomach. He grabs my ankle and yanks me back.

"Please, Rhydian, let me go," I plead. Kicking, my free foot lands in his hand, and he twists me onto my back, looming over me.

"You're hurting me!"

His eyes are full and imploring me as if he understands, but his mouth is a thin line.

I hear a whisper in his earpiece. An order. Whoever is giving it must be nearby because the whisper is echoed somewhere ahead of us. Eoin was right—someone is calling the shots, and Rhydian has taken me right to them.

Rhydian pulls me up by my arm, so we are both standing. His grip is tight. I recognize the familiar dirt, the earthy smell, and the fallen ceiling that I caused to rescue my father and Lucy. We are in the dungeon of the manor.

Rhydian isn't close enough for me to get that earpiece off him. A faint voice speaks to him through it, and he pushes me forward. The air around me shifts as someone transports near us. It's Tullen, and he has Abby.

"Abby . . . Tullen?"

Tullen taps his earpiece. "Both are here as requested. Rhydian and I will deliver the packages."

No.

Tullen pushes Abby forward ahead of me. Rhydian is at my back, blocking me from going anywhere but forward. We are guided down the stone stairs into the belly of the beast, the ancient dungeon. The sign announcing MacKinnon Manor looms overhead, swinging from its chains. There's a light source in the middle of the room beyond the doorway. I squint my eyes to see better. A male figure stands on a platform over a black liquid looking hole where the dungeon's floor should be. He waves his hands, and I watch the familiar designs glow on his hands and arms while a crown wavers over his head.

That is my magic, my familiar hum with someone else. It seems to waver toward me. A phantom rises out of the black hole and goes through the male figure. He grunts as if in pain, and the colors around him turn from bright light to a dull gray momentarily before becoming bright again. The phantoms take part of him when they emerge from the collapsed realm.

Is this how he controls them?

"Oh my Goddess, you have lost your mind," Abby sobs. She snatches her arm from Tullen. "What are you doing? Do you want to destroy Edayri?"

The man turns and walks down the stairs of the platform that hangs over the portal. He has a regal demeanor that makes my stomach sink when I see his face.

Mr. Boward.

"Thank you, Tullen. Take your post. Rhydian, guard our two hostile guests."

Rhydian pushes me forward so that I'm beside Abby and he stands behind both of us.

"What is your plan, father?" Abby asks, spitting his name.

A sinister laugh falls from Esmund's lips. "It is a simple mind that believes realms should be separated. I will collide them all. Rule over them. The Wiccan Queen supplies the power. Why should any of us fear the earthly planes? The Convergence is happening; it is no longer just conjecture. I simply found a way of speeding it up. Equality does not balance, but a merger and cleansing does."

"You're insane." My voice is loud. "Just because you have some power does not mean you will ever overcome the many who would oppose you. You won't succeed. All you are is a murderer and a thief."

He walks over to me, smirking, then smacks me hard. My head whips to the side. I taste the iron of blood in my mouth. Rhydian flinches in my peripheral vision.

"I succeeded in so many things leading up to this point, and you were oh-so willing. Duty is damned by the ignorance of youth. Do you want to whine some more about leaving normal behind? Don't worry. Your reign will be insignificant for another few minutes until your blood is spilled and your full magick released to me. The Boward family will become the royal family they were always meant to be."

The air shifts again. Esmund's eyes widen.

"Tsk, tsk," Evan says mockingly. "When Nuala broke your engagement, you were no longer part of the royal family, Esmund. Man, do you take a breakup hard. That was over two decades ago."

I peek behind Rhydian and see Quinn and Sabine with Evan. They use magick to hold back two Guardians around the portal. They move their hands and control light bolts and air.

"You bore me, Evan," Esmund coughs.

Esmund twists his hand, and Evan rises into the air. Evan twist midway like a gymnast, throwing out his arms, and light surrounds him. He gently lowers himself back to the ground before throwing a blast so severe that the platform crumbles into the portal.

"No!" Esmund reaches for it with magick, trying to stop it, but he's too late.

The portal ripples like a storm on water and pulls the structure into itself like a raging ocean, swallowing it whole. The screech of the phantoms outside of the dungeon makes everyone cower except Evan. He strides toward Esmund.

Evan gets the upper hand on Esmund, who recovers quickly. The pull of my magick from me to Esmund looks vaguely like a lightning bolt. Does he notice? The hum of my magick is still light but more present than before. Maybe I can use it to get that earpiece off Rhydian.

Esmund throws a large object that crashes where Evan was standing, but Evan disappears right in time. Tullen surveys the threats from beside Esmund and moves in to attack Sabine and Quinn.

The laugh that comes from Esmund is manic. He turns to Abby and me.

"Subdue them! They are subservient to our objective."

Rhydian pushes us to our knees.

"Son, it is almost time for the sacrifice. It must be her so that I can retain the Goddess gifts she is so unworthy of. Bring her here."

Abby moves in front of me. "No! You can't do this father. The blood vow! It will kill him! Father." Tears stream down her face.

"The blood vow might transfer to me, but even if it doesn't, we all make sacrifices—something you, Abigail, know nothing about! Rhydian has always known his duty. That is what makes him the best captain of the Guardians," Esmund says.

Evan comes up behind Tullen and boxes his ears. The earpiece flies off. Tullen turns in shock. Evan transports to another Guardian and does the same, one after another. They all shake their heads, clearing whatever spell was controlling them.

Esmund is not consistently giving orders; there must be someone else helping him. Rhydian doesn't acknowledge what Evan is doing behind Esmund. He pulls me up to stand. Abby grabs my hand, and Rhydian yanks me from her. He pushes me forward with his outstretched arm, a knife to my back.

Esmund is laughing. Abby pleads with her father, but when it yields no response, she spits at him. "Monster! You bastard."

Esmund's back is to us as he tries to repair the podium structure over the raging portal. My magick flows over his arms and wavers over his head.

I twist sharply to face Rhydian, putting my hand over his knife. Maybe I can influence him through his blood vow. My cheek still throbs from Esmund smacking my face.

"Rhydian, make your own choice. Pull away from your father's command."

He stares at my hand and the knife that now points at my stomach. Rhydian hears me. He is warring inside with what he's been commanded to do. He wants to protect me but doesn't have the freedom to do so, and it's tearing him apart.

"I can't." His worried eyes are at odds with his stoic warrior nature.

"But I can," I say. His fingers soften on the hilt and I hold him steady. I should be terrified, shaking, but I'm not. I'm resigned to what I need to do. I know how to break this control, how to get close enough to reach his ear.

The dungeon shakes and parts of the ceiling fall. Sabine is yelling, and the air moves with people transporting out of the dungeon.

I yank the knife forward into my stomach. The pain is instant and radiates all over my body. Rhydian catches me as I fall, unable to hold my own weight, and guides me to the ground. His eyes close; his lip trembles.

Our souls intermingle and rip. I reach my hand to his face and he leans into it, our faces not an inch from each other. Despite the roaring, burning pain in my body, the fact remains that Rhydian's hand went against his oath. The blood vow is broken.

I shock him with my lips on his and grab the earpiece, crushing and throwing it.

My hum rises faintly on my skin. "I love you."

"I failed you," he whispers, his forehead to mine.

I don't expect the welling tears in his storming eyes. He's back.

Tullen pulls Rhydian back from me, and it's as if limbs are being removed; both Rhydian and I scream in agony. Evan lays his hands on me before yanking the knife from my body, a pressure I barely register.

"Rhydian!" I yell.

"We're transporting," Evan says, and he gently picks me up. I grab his neck with my bloody hand.

Evan lays me on the ground beside Eoin at the front of the manor.

Eoin gasps. "Willow."

Evan's hand glows, and warmth eases my wound, so much so that I'm able to sit up. His demon horns shine in the twilight. He is quite powerful in his own right. My uncle just saved me. We've been here before, but this time we are not fighting each other. This time we are on the same side, fighting together. My mother would be so proud of him.

"I'd rather have your admiration than my dead sister's," Evan says.

"You read minds now?"

"No, but it's written all over your face. I'm just highly intuitive." He taps his temple. "Better?"

"Yes and no." My wound is healed, but—

The manor and the earth crumble around us. I hang on to both Evan and Eoin as we move away from the manor. The west side collapses into the dungeons with a massive groan. Smoke rises from the structure as stone and mortar fill the space below.

Silence.

I spot Cross with Rhydian near the collapsed part of the manor.

Several phantoms float around and dodge into the rubble. The portal is buried while the phantoms remain here.

A light ball hits Eoin square in the back, and he stumbles forward, carrying me with him. Evan rolls gracefully to the side and throws air toward the aggressor.

Quinn appears in front of us and drags Eoin to the side to heal him. Eoin holds Quinn's hand. I survey my surroundings quickly before I jump and roll to dodge a weak light ball from Esmund. Sabine attacks Esmund, her red hair wild behind her and her purple cloak rippling like a storm. She is fierce and powerful.

Esmund screeches in a tone that makes the phantoms rush toward him, but when they do, they go through him, and he crumples. They are no longer under his command.

The air moves and Emily transports in a lightning flash with Daniel. They are both in brass armor, Emily familiar with her eagle headdress.

Evan grabs me and we transport on top of the unsuspecting Esmund. Evan's hand is at his throat as he lifts him into the air. Esmund grasps at Evan's hand. He doesn't look so powerful anymore; he seems pale, fragile, and frightened.

"It's your bracelet, Willow! Remove it!" Evan commands.

I yank the silver elastic band from my wrist and call my magick. It flows freely. The warmth of the flow centers me. I'm home in myself again.

Esmund chokes and pulls on Evan's hands. "Call them," Evan sneers. He throws Esmund to the ground. It's like a beacon for the phantoms. They go through him over and over again. They are lost. Their portal is closed, and they are stuck here with no purpose. Their guide has tricked them, and they are angry.

Esmund screams with each pass as black blood wells and pours over his skin.

"Do you trust me?" Evan asks.

I nod. He grabs my hand, and I watch our magick

connect. My crown is glowing, my body whole and powerful, covered in my magick. Evan is covered in light too, his horns more prevalent and gleaming atop his head.

"Gather them. Push them into the vessel."

Somehow, Esmund finds the strength to crawl toward a sword lying near a fallen Guardian. Emily jumps on top of Esmund with her staff and sinks it into his stomach. Evan guides our magick to the staff, and the phantoms funnel through it into Esmund. When they've all gone, Emily raises her hands and lightning hits it. What was once Esmund is now a black hole. The staff is gone too, leaving only ash.

I'm being lifted in the air with Evan, our hands still together. His voice echoes in my mind. "Speak to them. Fulfill a new destiny."

"We stand together as a family and as Edayrians united—Goddess and Horned God."

Cheering erupts from most of the crowd below. Others are stunned in place.

"The fighting is over," Evan says in a booming voice.

Sabine is smiling at us as we come to the ground. Emily hugs me while Daniel watches everyone uneasily. I see Eoin and Quinn with their heads together. Tullen, Abby, and Cross are surrounding Rhydian, his head hung low and his shoulders shaking.

I make my way to Rhydian with Emily and Daniel in my wake. Cross taps Rhydian on his shoulder. He turns to me, and everyone moves off to give us some space. The beating of my heart feels off. My voice is paralyzed. We stare at one another, saying everything we can't say. It feels strange to no longer be in each other's mind.

"I—"

"Willow—"

I smile weakly. "I am sorry, Rhydian. I didn't know how else to release you from control—"

He won't look at me. He kicks the ground with his boot. "Willow, I knew he was doing something, I just didn't' know—I was complicit in duty to him. I broke the vow long before you forced me to. He helped me with the corsage." He shakes his head. "I never would have—"

He's taking the blame, but that is Rhydian for you. He wouldn't want me to blame myself. Another form of protection. I step forward, wanting to comfort him and wanting him to comfort me, but he steps back and holds his hands up. "Wait. I—"

"Rhydian. Please," I plead.

"I loved you, but I can't be here. I can't be what you need—"

I want to stop my tears from falling, but I can't. He loved me. Past tense. My heart crumbles; my feelings haven't changed. I want him. I want us. Not us duty-bound by a vow, but by love.

"I've got to go. You won't see me for—a time. I'll send in my resignation to Eoin."

"Please, don't go—alone." Take me with you, I plead with my eyes.

Rhydian looks over his shoulder at Tullen before turning back to me. "I won't."

"Can you do me one favor, and not as an order or command?" Rhydian flinches at my words. "Can you hold off on resigning? Take time, and please check in with Cross or Quinn when you can."

The weight of this moment, his eyes the color of the troubled ocean, and a picture of grief and torment are things I will never forget.

Rhydian closes the space between us and his lips crush mine. His hands are on my face pulling me closer, reaching beyond ourselves. I give in to him and cling to the hope that this isn't goodbye. In the most selfish way, I will it not to be, but not through my magick, just through the panic of my heart.

Rhydian pulls from me and puts his forehead to mine—a last connection before we step apart. There isn't one path, the right path; there is only our path. I know in my heart things between us aren't over permanently, but then again, my heart is hopeful even when it shouldn't be.

"Goodbye, Willow."

I let him go, and it kills me. I hug myself as I watch through my tears him walk to Tullen.

Abby squeezes my shoulder. "Willow?" She watches her brother, then jogs after him. "Wait! Wait, Rhydian!" He stops short, his back to her. "No! This isn't what you want, Rhydian. I know you love her. Father wasn't innocent. This is his own outcome. He would have sacrificed you and anyone to get power, and you know it!" she yells.

He walks away, never turning to face her. Abby's shoulders fall.

The fog on the ground seems to rise to the trees. Rhydian transports away with Tullen.

Eoin starts giving orders behind me to the Guardians with Cross and Thaxam. Bodies are transported to the Hallowed Hall. Death and blood are all around us, all for the normalcy I wanted so badly.

My vision is too blurry to recognize Emily in front of me, but I hear her voice as she holds my shoulders and says, "You are not alone, and you have not lost everything. You are not to blame, Willow."

"Why would you say that?"

"We may not have a blood vow, but I am your best friend. I know you, Willow."

I hug her and let my tears fall.

CHAPTER 27

Fourteen days later . . .

The sun provides welcoming warmth. I soak it up in my black robe, sitting tall in the white plastic chair with my ankles crossed. The grass tickles my feet through my wedge sandals.

The sounds from the stage and podium have become a blur over the last thirty minutes. My mind keeps wandering, replaying all that occurred in the days leading up to now, thinking about the mass funerals and honoring of heroes in a time of change in Edayri. The hum of my magick comforts me, along with the sense of freedom that came when Evan and I released Wiccan royal rule over Edayri from our family all together. The new legion council, the governing body in Edayri, was appointed for its inaugural year. After a full term of three years, an election will be held for the replacement of its members.

The establishment of a militarized police body has

been appointed by the legion council and guided by General Ax and Commander Eoin. A charter has been drafted for equalized laws of no harm toward others. Evan and I are no more than figureheads of a royal family and more commonly seen as directed decedents of the Horned God and the Goddess. The idea of a different future here in the Terra realm isn't something I dwell on anymore. This is my life. I turn and see Sabine, Eoin, Quinn, Cross, Thaxam (substantially disguised), and Evan sitting in the riser seats.

I let my mind wander to Rhydian. I haven't spoken to or heard from him since we said goodbye at the manor's ruins. The text message I got from Tullen was brief, but they are okay. They are traveling, not staying put in one place for very long. Tullen revealed that Rhydian is beginning a search for his mother.

My mental fog dissipates when Ms. Chin introduces Lucy, our class valedictorian. Lucy joins her on the stage. Her smile is pasted, her handshake formal. I don't recognize Lucy as my best friend anymore. We haven't spoken much, and when we have, it's not meaningful. She is pulling away from me, but maybe I am doing the same. She approaches the podium and pulls index cards from a pocket in her robe.

Lucy is rejecting the part of herself that I once rebelled against. She and Emily barely speak anymore. I imagine she'll head to the west coast and begin college life we always talked about. I'm happy for her.

"Seniors, today is the day that begins your future. Your hard work, planning, and partying—" a few jocks holler in support, garnering laughs from everyone "—

have provided you with a skill set that will grow and expand as you carry it with you on your next adventure. You have choices and know that you can change your mind. Change it frequently, for that matter. Now is the time to stumble and find your way. Find the person you were meant to be without the labels of who you are expected to be. Define who you are by living and trying—"

I'm proud of Lucy. I miss her and cherish our past friendship. Daniel isn't here, and Emily hasn't shared much about his whereabouts. I haven't pressed it. Marco and Emily sit next to each other a few rows ahead.

Ms. Chin begins the procession of students to receive their diplomas. It's the start of an independent life for so many, and all I recognize is the absence of what was—of my mother, Mrs. Scott, my father, and Rhydian.

I'm toward the end of the procession, and when I walk back to my seat, I can't help but be grateful. Despite it all, I'm here, and my family is expanding. The unwanted is my new normal, and it's growing on me.

Ms. Chin approaches the podium and clears her throat. "Ladies and gentlemen, I now present to you the graduating class of Trinity Cross!"

In celebration with my fellow classmates, I throw my graduation cap high into the sky. Everyone is smiling and laughing.

The sky ripples unnaturally with purple and blue. A loud clap of thunder makes me jump before lightning streaks across the sky followed by another significant boom. The sound echoes over the crowd. To everyone around me it's the start of a storm. To me and everyone from Edayri, it's a warning.

The Convergence has begun.

THE KNOT SPELL
WICCAN ROYAL SCEPTER

By knot of one, the spell's begun
By knot of two, it cometh true
By knot of three, so mote it be
By knot of four, this power I store
By knot of five, the spell's alive
By knot of six, this spell I fix
By knot of seven, events I'll leaven
By knot of eight, it will be fate
By knot of nine, what's done is mine

AUTHOR'S NOTE

Book reviews matter.

Please leave a review where you buy and/or review books, so that this book can be discovered by readers just like you. Thank you for your support.

ACKNOWLEDGMENTS

To my editor, Spencer Hamilton, for your push and encouragement to revisit this series. Reign would not exist without you and I'm super proud of this story.

For Writer's Atelier and my Write Gym mates, especially our leader and coach Racquel Henry, thank you for the ongoing unwavering support and the gentle accountability check-in's.

To Maria Spada for making covers so beautiful that people have to pick them up.

To first readers Janelle Gabay, Allison Newell, and C.T. Jones. Your input was crucial in crafting this story and making it shine.

To my family and friends, thank you for being there and for understanding when I haven't been there. Butch, Allison, and Danielle, your love and support is everything to me.

Lastly, to all the readers who bring books into their hearts and breathe life into them with every page's turn, thank you for joining the journey with me, the ride has just started.

ALSO BY C. M. NEWELL

The Unwanted Series

Magick

Reign

Sacred

For more details please go to the author website:

www.AuthorCMNewell.com

ABOUT THE AUTHOR

C. M. Newell is an award-winning YA fantasy author, receiving the 2016 New Apple Fantasy Award for her debut novel Magick in The Unwanted Series.

C. M. is a lover of all things fantasy and fairytale, especially the twisted ones. She loves to write strong female characters who don't fall victim to circumstance but instead rise above. She prefers a world where a princess can save herself.

Originally from Tennessee and a nomad from various states and countries, C. M. now calls home to sunny Florida with her family.

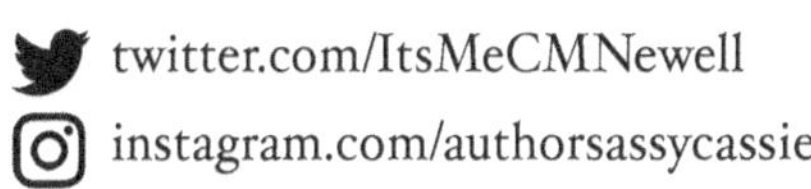

twitter.com/ItsMeCMNewell

instagram.com/authorsassycassie